The
Missing
Hydrangeas

Also by Eileen M. Berger
in Large Print:

The Coin Conspiracy

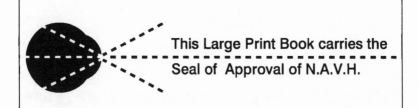

CHURCH CHOIR MYSTERIES™

The Missing Hydrangeas

Eileen M. Berger

Thorndike Press • Waterville, Maine

Published in 2003 by arrangement with
Guideposts Book Division.

Thorndike Press® Large Print Paperback.

The tree indicium is a trademark of Thorndike Press.

The text of this Large Print edition is unabridged.
Other aspects of the book may vary from the original edition.

Set in 16 pt. Plantin by Al Chase.

Printed in the United States on permanent paper.

Library of Congress Cataloging-in-Publication Data

Berger, Eileen M.
    The missing hydrangeas / Eileen M. Berger.
        p. cm. — (Church choir mysteries)
    ISBN 0-7862-5811-X (lg. print : sc : alk. paper)
    1. Choirs (Music) — Fiction.   2. Cats — Fiction.
    3. Large type books.   I. Title.   II. Series.
PS3552.E7183M47 2003
    813'.54—dc21   2003056350

*This book is dedicated with love to
Conrad, Sarah and Leslie,
our children-in-love
who are not only the chosen, loving spouses
of Vickie, Jim and Bill
and wonderful parents to our
seven grandchildren,
but are also fine, outstanding Christians
and a joy to Bob and me — as well as to their
many friends.*

As the Founder/CEO of NAVH, the only national health agency solely devoted to those who, although not totally blind, have an eye disease which could lead to serious visual impairment, I am pleased to recognize Thorndike Press* as one of the leading publishers in the large print field.

Founded in 1954 in San Francisco to prepare large print textbooks for partially seeing children, NAVH became the pioneer and standard setting agency in the preparation of large type.

Today, those publishers who meet our standards carry the prestigious "Seal of Approval" indicating high quality large print. We are delighted that Thorndike Press is one of the publishers whose titles meet these standards. We are also pleased to recognize the significant contribution Thorndike Press is making in this important and growing field.

Lorraine H. Marchi, L.H.D.
Founder/CEO
NAVH

* Thorndike Press encompasses the following imprints: Thorndike, Wheeler, Walker and Large Pr int Press.

Chapter One

"I'm ready for a rest," Gracie Parks stated, dropping down onto the old stone wall fronting Molly Maginnis's yard.

"Sure you are." Her eighty-year-old uncle was taking his seat much more carefully. "You power-walk five miles in little over an hour, yet you're ready to sit down twice just coming these few blocks from Main Street!"

"Well, my praise-and-power walk is first thing in the morning, Uncle Miltie — just me, all by myself — no talkin', just walkin'."

George Morgan couldn't keep the twinkle from those eyes of his, which still missed very little. "Maybe you've put your finger on my problem — I try to do both at the same time, and end up winded."

He was a good eighteen years older than Gracie, and had always been her favorite uncle. She'd thought she was doing *him* a favor, inviting him to come live with her three years ago, after Aunt Doris died, but it had proved to be just as much of a blessing for her. "Look at those blue hydrangeas there at the end of Molly's walk! Aren't they gorgeous?"

"No more so than yours, my girl. In fact I'd say *yours* are even a little darker, a more intense blue."

"Ah, but you're not the judge, unfortunately." She sighed, not sure if his saying that was mostly loyalty or if he really did believe hers to be superior. "What's your guess as to how many awards Molly's going to win again on Friday?"

"Who knows?" He shrugged broadly. "Sometimes I wonder about those judges at our county fair."

She herself had quite a few opinions on that topic, but what was the use of her complaining? Instead, she called across the street, giving the woman baby-sitting two small grandchildren a compliment on how well they seemed to get along, and how cute they were.

Uncle Miltie, first called that because friends of another era had considered his jokes to be as bad as those of the then-extremely-popular Milton Berle, wasn't ready to change topics. "Don't you give up, Gracie. With you and Marge and Rich having worked so hard on your own hydrangeas these last years, we're gonna see surprises this time."

He pushed back up onto his feet and positioned himself behind his wheel-fronted walker. "Come on, lazybones, let's get going."

"You're a hard taskmaster, begrudging your own niece a bit of rest." She tried to look and sound irritated as she stood up, then nodded toward the lawn. "Molly should use some of her energy on mowing grass, rather than concentrating on just one variety of flowers."

He was moving forward behind his walker, but paying attention to other things. "She should *especially* do something about that ugly shell of a building over there."

She agreed. "What was it — your first year in Willow Bend when fire destroyed her garage roof and wooden doors? I assumed she'd rebuild it — then I was sure she'd have those cement block walls torn down when she had the new garage built against the house like that."

Proceeding as slowly as they were, Gracie had probably not taken more than a hundred steps when the SUV pulled up beside them. "Anyone want a lift?"

"Nope, we're doing fine just as we are." Uncle Miltie didn't sound at all grateful for the offer made by Rick Harding, the computer whiz who sang tenor in the church

9

choir. "When I take a woman out for a walk, young man, I take that woman for a *walk*. None of that half-way shifting of gears in my makeup."

Rick grinned. "At least you get to take a lovely woman for a walk. . . ."

"Look, had you really wanted to help, you should have come sooner, not wait till we're practically home."

"Too bad about that." His warm, brown eyes betrayed amusement. "And here I was, coveting the pleasure of your company."

Gracie, leaning over to talk through the window, said, "We were just admiring Molly's hydrangeas."

"I haven't given up hope, though," he informed her, "and you'd better not, either. We've followed each and every one of those entry instructions, and we're going to put our very best flowers out there for inspection and judging.

"And, were I a betting man, I'd bet on *one* of us winning."

Gracie thought Rick was going to leave it there, but as he shifted gears and started to ease forward, his voice drifted back to them, ". . . At least *some*thing."

"Hunh!" Uncle Miltie snorted. "You shouldn't settle for just a 'something' for all your work and troubles. I'd want an award, a *real* prize — perhaps a loving cup." He rolled his eyes as he countered his own suggestion, "Too bad it's a slender check instead of a fat one."

They were both aware that the first-prize winner received only a blue ribbon and fifteen dollars, and that public affirmation for growing "the best" was really what the competitors were seeking. He looked around again while raising the back of the walker just enough so the front wheels could roll as he took another step forward. "No matter what those judges decide, Gracie, this interest in hydrangea-growing has done a lot to brighten up our part of town. First Molly, then Marge, and now you."

"And Rick across town, and the church and the parsonage." Gracie was pleased at her uncle's pointing out the improvement this had made. "It's good to know that a bit of a challenge — a bit of *rivalry*, even — can have such excellent results. We'd all been too busy with one thing or another to keep our gardens at their best, and we needed a spur."

"Yeah." He took a few more steps. "Just so that rivalry's kept within proper bounds."

"Agreed. And I assume you know all of us well enough by now not to be concerned about that kind of problem."

"That goes without saying, my dear," he told her, grinning.

It was almost second nature for Gracie to check the answering machine when entering her house, and today was no exception. The first message was from Barb Jennings, their church organist and choir director, asking that her call be returned. Gracie felt like ignoring that, since it might well be about how the Eternal Hope choir had not sounded as good as usual when singing last Sunday's anthem.

In principle, it had seemed a good idea to bring in some of these highfalutin' anthems, to give variety and to stretch the limits of what people already knew and loved — but Barb couldn't seem to get it through her head that many of the singers still could not read music.

Some of them had been part of the choir forever, or that's how it seemed. They could differentiate whether notes went up or down on the staffs, but how *much* difference that should make in pitch still was pretty much guesswork. Or they depended on the persons next to them, meaning either both were right or both wrong.

And no matter how often those rest symbols had been explained, it still took going over a piece again and again for them to know when to begin singing. It also required patience on the part of those who could actually read music and had true enough tones that the others could at least follow.

The second call, whatever its nature, was bound to be more pleasurable — or so she hoped. But the recorded voice and manner of her friend Rocco Gravino seemed overly serious when stating, "I've got a problem, Gracie, and need your help."

Rocky had become a strong and reliable friend through the years — even though her late husband, Elmo, often had regarded the newspaper editor as a thorn in his side.

But that was because of professional differences, for goodness sake! The much-mourned Elmo Parks had been the soul of integrity, and done his very best when he was mayor and sanitation expert and controller and, occasionally, when their Eternal Hope Church was temporarily without a minister, he even took over many of those responsibilities. Rocky Gravino was, in his own way, equally conscientious. As owner and editor of the only daily paper in the area, he had arrived in Willow Bend determined both personally and professionally to keep on top of whatever might be going on.

And to put it in his newspaper.

That's where the rub came in as far as Elmo was concerned. "Things get reported too soon," he'd complain. "We're still in the talking stage and trying to work out what's best under known circumstances, and to reach a consensus — then people get all riled up from too-eager or incomplete information. They choose sides from which they'll never, ever budge, even if proven wrong."

Gracie had not talked with Rocky for far too long. Hoping he might have a few minutes to visit in addition to explaining what kind of help he needed, she sat down on a kitchen chair and punched in the number for his personal phone at the *Gazette*.

Disappointed to hear a busy signal, Gracie knew just how to fill this free moment. Going over to the large white ironstone tureen her mother had always used as a cookie jar, she removed one of the last chocolate chip cookies from her baking several days earlier. She enjoyed trying new recipes, but Uncle Miltie, though willing to eat whatever "experiment" she made, still preferred the old recipes of his mother and wife.

The very small voice in her mind telling her she didn't need these additional calories

— that she was already a good twenty-five pounds over what the chart in the doctor's office designated "big bone" for a woman five feet four inches tall was successfully squelched. Again.

After all, she was on the go almost all the time, and needed sustenance.

And she'd faithfully done her walking today. As she almost always did.

The cookies, made with oatmeal and whole-wheat flour and nuts, were excellent, even if she did say so herself. And they were even more nutritious since she'd also dumped lots of powdered milk into the batter; she'd started doing that back when their son had gone through that stage of refusing to drink milk. He hadn't known until he was full-grown that he'd enjoyed its benefits in his mother's delicious meat loaf, biscuits and brownies. So she continued adding it now, especially since Uncle Miltie arrived. After all, she didn't want either of them to develop osteoporosis, as her mother had, causing her to stoop as she got older, and eventually to have that broken hip. And, another time, a broken wrist.

So, taking the last bite, *this is sort of a health food when one looks at it the right way. Unfortunately* — *or fortunately, as the case may be* — *I can't quite convince myself of its*

15

claims to being called that, but, still, it's sort of fun to try.

She punched the redial button, but got only the busy signal again. Trying one more time after sweeping the kitchen floor, she finally heard his voice on the other end. "Hi, Mr. Editor, you've been keeping yourself scarce."

"Good morning, Gracie. Or, I should say, I *hope* it's being a good one for you."

"Everything's fine here." But he didn't sound as upbeat as he usually was with her. "It's not that way for you?"

"Well, it's nothing absolutely earth-shaking-horrible," he admitted, using an expression he would never have tolerated in writing from one of his staff. "I got a call from Jennie Pentz just before trying to get you. You know she and her sister started that catering service two summers ago . . . ?"

"Of course; and they do a good job." *They were working at it before I ever started my own cooking for hire.*

"Yes, they do — though I personally prefer yours."

"Ah, so you *do* want something, handing out a compliment like that." She kept her voice light, teasing.

"Hey, I've told you before that you're fabulous at catering — but you've always said

16

you prefer serving only up to about fifty sit-down meals. Right?"

"Guilty as charged." She laughed. "And now, as to your problem?"

"Well, it seems that their mother's been having a lot of physical difficulties this past month. And she's now scheduled for open-heart surgery in Chicago tomorrow, which is just one day before they're committed to serving our Rotary Club dinner."

"Okay."

A tiny pause. "Okay — *what?*"

"Okay, I think I can help out — but please excuse my presumption if that wasn't what you were about to ask."

"Gracie, my friend, you are a lifesaver!" His sigh was comically over-dramatic. "I was afraid I'd have to call everyone and tell them it's been canceled, and now I find that I *do* have time to put out today's paper."

"Well-l-l, now you'd better tell me what I've got myself into. . . ."

Sixty-four reservations was the figure he gave her. "At least your menu isn't too complicated, and the ham and the stuffed chicken-breast halves don't require too much last-moment fixing," she reassured him.

"Yeah, and it's in your church. . . ."

"It is? That will make things much easier.

17

For that matter, I can ask the men to help set up the tables tomorrow after choir practice." But then she asked, "Did they say what they'd promised for dessert, or anything else?"

"Not that I know of — and, under these circumstances, anything you want to make will be fine."

"Oh, good!" She couldn't resist teasing him with, "Then I can get away with a bunch of box-cakes."

There was dead silence for a moment before, "Well, if that's what you want — or if you're running out of time, or something. . . ."

She laughed. "You're a good sport, Rocky." She was carrying her portable phone, filling a cup with tap water and carrying it over to put in the microwave. "There may be one or two of those, but I promise you'll have at least two kinds of pie, as well."

"What a relief! You know from experience that I *love* cherry and blueberry pie — especially yours."

"Rocky?" There were other things she needed to find out. "When is this meal scheduled to be served?"

"At six, if possible. Though, if you need a bit more time, people could wait in the sanctuary — or somewhere."

She realized even as she shook her head what he hoped she would say. "Six will be no problem."

Gracie chose a tea bag from her mother's old sugar bowl and got the loose-leaf notebook from beside her favorite cookbooks. As soon as the microwave beeped, she got her cup of hot water and started steeping her tea. She had been working on the menu for only a few minutes before she got up to make another call.

Jennie Pentz sounded apprehensive as she picked up the phone on its first ring, so Gracie tried to reassure her by saying, "It's just me, Gracie. Rocky just told me about your mother's surgery and I am so sorry it's become necessary."

"It's such a *shock* — I haven't seen her for over a week, but talked with her on the phone at least every day or so. She's told me she was feeling awful tired, but she never even mentioned her chest pain."

"Did those pains come and go?"

"I guess so — apparently even Dad had no idea it was more than muscle pain from coughing until during the night, when he insisted on taking her to the emergency room. The EKG they did there shows that she's already had *one* heart attack and, well, other tests confirm that she needs immediate surgery."

"That's being done in the same hospital?"

"Um-hm. They've got her scheduled at one o'clock tomorrow."

Gracie recognized the near-panic in her voice. "Look, is there anything I can help with here — so you can get away?"

"Well, I was just about to call Anderson's Meat Market — I hope I can cancel our order there — and my sister and I feel just terrible about not being able to keep our promise to the Rotary Club."

"Jennie?" Gracie interrupted. "Look, Jennie, Rocky understands, and so do I, of course, and I told him I could help you out with this." *I hope she'll understand I'm not trying to take away business from her.* ". . . That is, if you'd like me to."

There was not a moment's hesitation before, "Oh, would you, Gracie? Lori and I would be most grateful!"

In short order, Gracie had both agreed to take responsibility for picking up and using the meat that had been ordered, and learned that nothing else had been purchased yet. But then Jennie added, "One of the women from your church, Louise McCall, agreed to make two shoo-fly pies and two coconut custard ones, and April Peru was to prepare fresh-from-the-oven rolls right before dinner — but I can cancel those."

"Were you picking them up, or were they being delivered?"

"They're to be brought to the church around five or five-thirty."

"Great! We'll leave those as they are — or should we let them know I'd appreciate their doing as planned?"

"I — I'd better call one of them, and ask her to notify the other."

"If you're sure you want to take time for that." *But Jennie probably feels the need to keep good relationships there if she wants these women to bake for her other times.* "In the meantime, how about my putting this on our prayer chain?"

"Oh, would you?" There was unmistakable gratitude there — followed by a frustrated, "And I never even *thought* to do that for mine. But when I call April, I'll ask her to take care of that as well as notifying Louise."

Uncle Miltie came into the kitchen as Gracie was on the phone with Estelle Livett, her fellow church-choir member who was also chairperson of Eternal Hope Community Church's prayer chain. His awareness of their concern was obvious as he stood there by the table, head bowed.

When she filled him in about her being in charge of the Thursday evening dinner, however, he fretted, "You're sure you can get enough help on such short notice?"

"I'm going to start calling my usual people right now." She was disappointed to find that two of them had other plans, but then she tried Tish and Tyne, the Turner twins, as they were still known throughout the church and community even though they were now Tish Ball and Tyne Anderson. These thirty-five-year-old sisters had been almost inseparable in their early years — and even now, each with her own husband, family, and house, they usually participated together in all their Willow Bend involvements.

They often seemed even to think alike. But this time Tish agreed to help with food preparation and serving, with Tyne indicating she'd rather not. She was, however, willing to bake three apple and two blueberry pies for Gracie — and even to produce one of her famed macadamia nut sheet cakes.

Gracie was still unable to get a response when ringing back Barb Jennings. So she left a message that she was driving to the church to check things in the kitchen, but would soon return home.

Pastor Paul Meyer was just pulling out of the parking lot as she arrived, and they greeted each other through their open car windows. "Hi, Gracie! I just now heard from Estelle that as of now you're in charge of our Rotary dinner tomorrow night."

She grinned wryly. "*That* wasn't meant as part of the prayer request I gave her."

"It isn't — at least as far as I know. She knew I'd be interested in knowing you're doing that because of Lori's and Jennie's mother." His smile was approving. "Right now, I'm starting out to make a couple of visits to parishioners in nursing homes."

She called after him, "I know how pleased they'll be to see you!"

Her arms were filled as she entered the back door, for she'd decided to bring her better quality paper plates, as well as other disposable items, rather than bothering with them later when things would probably be more hectic. How she appreciated the convenience of her church's splendid kitchen, with its large ovens and counter-top burners!

She used to take its amenities for granted, but from catering around this whole area, she had discovered that few other churches seemed to have very well-organized kitchens — unless they went in for making much of their money by serving meals.

Gracie turned on each of the burners and ovens, and also checked the temperature of the refrigerator and freezer. She was grateful to find that each appliance seemed to be functioning perfectly.

After getting out a clean hand towel, along with a dishcloth and towel, she gathered up a few that appeared used and started out the doorway toward her car — and stopped short.

The hydrangeas flanking this rear exit — the large pink and blue peegees on either side of lower, flatter hill-of-snow white ones — looked odd. Someone had snipped off most of the flowers! Had they been that way before she'd come in perhaps a half-hour ago? She'd been carrying all those boxes, could she have failed to notice something this horrible?

Checking more closely, she saw that, in fact, the bushes were almost entirely denuded and that all of what had been cut off — flower heads, leaves and branches — had been removed from the scene of the crime. *This is ridiculous! Why would anyone cut off all those beautiful blooms? There were far too many removed for anyone to have stolen to use in vases for their homes.* It was beyond vandalism, really, she thought, remembering her own cherished hydrangeas — in fact, it was almost like murder, she decided.

And she shuddered.

Chapter Two

Gracie stopped at the Willow Mart on her way home; she'd expected to do the major shopping the next day for Thursday's dinner, but she did need a loaf of bread, some milk, and laundry bleach.

Picking up a free copy of *Willow Bend's Shopper and News* at the front of the store, she stood at the beginning of aisle one to glance through it for any specials she should look for here at the Mart. Lettuce and carrots were both on sale, as well as her favorite brand of ranch-style salad dressing. As all of the vegetables were especially fresh-looking, she decided also to buy cabbages for coleslaw. These would keep as well in her own refrigerator as here at the store.

It was almost noon when she arrived home, so she quickly made chicken-and-corn soup, using leftover meat and broth, along with two hard-boiled eggs and a can of cream-style corn. "It's as good as always," Uncle Miltie complimented her as he got to his feet again. "Another of those wonderful soups that, with a few crackers, make a full meal."

It was a pleasure cooking for this man — as it had been for Elmo, both of them being generous with their praise. "I'm glad you enjoy it. It's one of my favorites, too."

He started for the back door. "I'm going out and check things before the rain comes."

She was still clearing the table, and puzzling over the mystery of the mutilated plants, something she had neglected to tell her uncle about, when the phone rang. It was Barb, sounding even more upset than usual. "Am I glad you're back, Gracie!"

"I tried to get you when I returned from the church, but. . . ."

"I'm so upset." She was obviously not paying attention to Gracie's words. "Something awful's happened!"

"I'm sorry, dear. What's the matter?"

"It's my hydrangeas!"

What a relief! I was afraid someone had died or something. "What's wrong?"

"Oh, Gracie, you should *see* them — almost all the flowers have been cut off, and the bushes look terrible."

Gracie had a mental image of the ones she had just seen at the church, but her desire was to handle this calmly. "The ones at the

27

end of your front walk?"

"Those and the ones by the flagpole in the side yard."

"Is it — just the flowers, or are the bushes damaged?"

"Mostly it's the flowers — not just the petals, mind you, but good-sized chunks of the stems are gone, too."

Just like at the church! "When did it happen?"

"I don't *know*." It was almost a wail. "They were fine yesterday evening — I'm sure they were! But when I went outside this morning, there they were! All cut back. *Ruined*."

Gracie figured it was time to tell Barb about the bushes at the church. But, naturally, hearing that only upset her more. She lowered her voice, as if someone might overhear. "Maybe there are devil-worshippers around here, or some satanic cult is attacking our church. And . . . and me, too, since I'm the organist and choir director. Oh, Gracie!"

"I really doubt that, Barb." *But what good is my saying that when I have no better suggestion to offer?*

"Well, it makes me mad, as well as scared," Barb went on. "After all, those deep pink ones by my walk were huge this

28

year — and every single bloom was as perfect as any in the gardening magazines and catalogs! I had a good chance at that blue ribbon this year!"

"I know," Gracie sympathized, inwardly wondering, as she often did, how Barb could be so impossibly single-minded. Eventually she was able to bring the conversation to other things, including Jennie's mother's emergency surgery, and Gracie's taking on the Rotary dinner.

"It's good of you to step in like that, Gracie," Barb was gracious enough to tell her. "Do you have plenty of people to help?"

"I think so — hope so, anyway. And right now there's not an awful lot for any others to take care of. As for myself, I did get some shopping done today."

Gracie was putting a cookbook back on the shelf when Marge Lawrence, her next-door neighbor and best friend, came to the kitchen door, already talking as she walked in. "Uncle Miltie told me you were in here trying to find a recipe that you'd know was different from the same old thing — but one that even the most critical old so-and-so couldn't find fault with."

"He knows how to get to the heart of a

matter, doesn't he?" Gracie laughed. "I hadn't thought of it in those terms, but he's right — I do enjoy varying the seasonings I use or adding my own special 'mystery ingredients.'

"But you know how it is around here. They jump to the conclusion something's wrong with the salad dressing or the chicken dumplings if I liven it up with anything even slightly unfamiliar."

"Well," Marge lifted the lid of the ironstone tureen and removed a chocolate chip cookie, "just don't fool around with the recipe for this or your other fabulous treats."

Gracie joined her at the kitchen table, secretly amused that even this woman who often catered with her had no idea that her cookies seldom were made exactly the same way. Sometimes she added peanut butter, or tiny marshmallows or, if she had leftover nuts of any variety, they, too, might end up in the dough. And after Easter, the special chocolate left from coating her six dozen peanut-butter-and-marshmallow eggs was broken up and included in her next batch of cookies.

She shared with Marge her planned menu for the Rotary dinner. "So tell me, am I missing anything — besides more pies and at least one extra sheet cake?"

"Sounds great to me. I wish I could be there."

You probably do. At this time last year you were dating Landon Murphy, but. . . . "You could join, you know; there must be at least eight or ten women who are now members of our Rotary Club."

"I know, and I have been invited, but that's not the same as going as someone's date. It just isn't!"

Or as someone's wife! But Gracie wasn't about to dwell on that! Nor would she mention that she'd turned down invitations from both Abe Wasserman and Rocky Gravino. "Just for the sake of being with all those people who'd enjoy having you there, Gracie," was how Abe had put it when she hesitated.

She would certainly know everyone there, and she had every reason to believe she'd have a good time if she went with him. But, as she told him, "If we do that even *once,* before the next sundown the gossips of Willow Bend will have us in the midst of a torrid romance!"

Here in her own kitchen, on this lovely day, she just shrugged. "Life would be so much simpler if we didn't have to make decisions, wouldn't it? But really, Marge, I think you should reconsider becoming a member."

"I will — if *you* join, too." Her eyes were bright with anticipation.

Gracie shook her head. "At this point in my life I have no desire to tie up every Monday night like that."

"Why don't you give it a try? I'll bet you'd have such a good time that it would be worth going each week."

She wished her friend didn't keep trying to talk her into things. Yet she knew it was a tactic Marge often employed with the customers at her little gift shop. If she pressed just a little harder, she frequently was able to convince people to make those purchases they weren't sure about. Almost resenting any sales tactic being used on her, however, Gracie picked up her pen and straightened the paper in front of her. "No, thanks. Even if it might be the right thing for you."

She'd deliberately chosen to look busy, and it worked. Marge left in a few minutes. Gracie outlined on her pad all the things she could think of that needed to be done, then numbered them as to their importance.

As it turned out, she made sure to mow the lawn first, since the weatherman had predicted rain. Her house stood on a corner lot, and there were multiple plantings that took up quite a bit of space, so the job required careful maneuvering around them.

Uncle Miltie seldom grumbled anymore about her doing this, although she suspected it still bothered him. "That was always my job at home," he used to complain. "Let me at least hire one of the neighborhood boys, or one of the church youth."

"But I enjoy doing it," she would insist. "And it's not like your big suburban property, Uncle Miltie. I can finish this in an hour."

It was a good thing that was all the time it took, for quickly the clouds had begun rolling in. She was in the living room when the first flash of lightning struck. She couldn't help but sigh when she realized that she'd automatically turned off the sweeper and headed for the room that had been her husband's study. *Will I ever get over thinking of you as so very much alive, Elmo? Like now, when I started for your office to unplug your no-longer-there computer?*

Yet she was quite aware that she'd never want to forget him and their many years together. Yes, there was still sadness here, and regret — but she had such wonderful memories! *I'd never want to give up even one of those, Elmo — our love, our working together, our sharing of thoughts, dreams, ambitions, bodies.*

She walked briskly back to the sweeper and finished cleaning the carpet. She had that list of tasks lying there on the kitchen table, and this was only the third item she could check off.

Uncle Miltie had taken his shower between two of the afternoon thunderstorms and was now relaxing in his recliner with *National Geographic* when the lights first flickered, then went out. The electricity was still off when it was time for the evening meal, and he made no complaints when Gracie told him, "We're having sort of a weird supper, but I don't want to let out any of the cold air by opening the refrigerator or freezer doors.

"This cornstarch pudding I made just before the power went off shouldn't be left out in the warm like this."

He smiled as he looked at the two single servings of dessert at each of their places. "This brings back good memories of when I was growing up on the farm, before electricity was available in our valley.

"Most of our milk was sent to the creamery in big metal cans, but we'd save out two gallons each day for family use — more than that if we were having a lot of company, or making homemade ice cream, of course. The milk was put in crocks each morning, and those were set in the running water within the springhouse.

"Each of us usually drank a glass of it with each meal but sometimes, particularly in midsummer when we often had iced tea for dinner and supper, we'd end up having too much milk left — in which case Mom would often make a big batch of cornstarch pudding and serve it in soup bowls."

She recognized the soft light of reminiscing in his eyes, so only nodded, encouraging him to continue. "I remember this as happening most frequently for Sunday lunch," he went on. "We'd come home from church and change clothes, then eat the pudding even before going out to gather eggs."

Her mother had mentioned this, too. "It sounds like an excellent idea — especially for grandma's sake. This would have given her at least a little free time in her busy schedule."

"Umm, this tastes exactly like hers." He was savoring his first spoonful. "Yes, Mother did keep very busy, as we all did. But she certainly knew how to celebrate a Sabbath day!

"Even when we had company, which was very often, there was always Sunday School and church in the morning, of course, but then the afternoons were spent as a family, playing croquet in the big side yard, or walking back through the fields and going across the South Creek bridge, and walking through the woods."

His voice gradually faded away as his memory focused not on the kitchen wall but on those days of seven decades or more ago.

She sat motionless there at the table until he sighed, looked down at the empty dish in front of himself and replaced it with his other helping. Little more was said until after the meal. It was while he was getting to his feet and reaching for his walker that he said, "Those Depression days must have been extremely difficult for our parents, but I can't imagine how they could have been better as far as we kids were concerned."

Could Arlen say that about his growing up with Elmo and me, here in Willow Bend? We both wanted more children, but for some reason weren't able to have them. But we did the best we could: our home was always open to neighborhood kids, and we had scads of them here. For that matter, this was the only house on the block where everyone was welcome — and how they did come!

The sky was still leaden, and the house as dark as though the sun had been set for an hour. They didn't often lose their electricity in Willow Bend, Indiana, but it had still not come on when they went to bed early, around 9:30. Gracie and her uncle had spent the evening at the kitchen table, playing Scrabble by the light of the old kerosene lamp she kept primarily for sentimental reasons, since it had belonged to her grandparents.

The darkness inspired Uncle Miltie to share one of his "light bulb" jokes while turning over the Scrabble tiles. "How many jugglers does it take to screw in a light bulb? Just one, but it takes three light bulbs." Gracie couldn't help laughing thinking about a juggler in their dark kitchen.

Scrabble was Uncle Miltie's favorite game, and he never seemed to forget any of those seldom-used-in-conversation words like *qua,* or *iamb,* or *hyson* — this latter (which the dictionary proved to be a type of Chinese green tea just as he said) being the one with which he won the third game by adding the *hy* and *o* to the other two letters already on the board.

"My ego can't stand another game with you tonight," she pretend-grumbled while gathering the lettered blocks together and putting them back in the familiar box.

He was obviously trying to control his victor's grin while reminding her, "Hey, you won the second one."

"Yep, I do get lucky occasionally." But they both knew, in fact, they were quite evenly matched.

She placed the lamp turned down low, on the stand at the end of the living room and suggested that they keep their doors open in case they needed to get up during the night. Another brief thunderstorm arrived shortly after Gracie got in bed, but she slept through any that might have come later.

There was still no electricity when she got up in the early morning, pulled on sweatpants and shirt, and prepared to start out for her brisk morning walk. *I'm not going to let myself worry about preparations for that dinner tomorrow. We still have time — and the power's sure to come back on this morning.*

Quickly, however, she learned that she *did* have something to worry about — when she received a frantic call from Marge. Her friend was weeping into the phone. She had just found her hydrangeas *decapitated* — as she called what had been done to her plants. "I never really expected to win at the county fair, Gracie, not like Barb — but I *liked* those flowers! And I followed all of Uncle Miltie's advice about adding acid or ammonia to make the pinks pinker and the blues bluer."

"I know you did, and they are — were beautiful." She stood still there for a moment before saying, "I'm coming right over."

She replaced the phone and stepped outside into the sunny, sparkling, washed-clean world, then realized she'd have to go around by the walk instead of crossing the lawns on the grass, as usual. Otherwise, her sneakers would be sodden within the first ten feet.

Her cat, Gooseberry, obviously had no such concerns, and his pumpkin-colored body was soon glistening with moisture. He stayed more or less near her — that is, if she counted alongside or in front or back or, sometimes, even nearly tripping her. "Goose!" she scolded, nearly stumbling, "Watch where you're going!"

He appeared to ignore her — except for that little twitch of his right ear, which elicited a slight upturn to the corner of her own lips. But her grin lasted only a second, for she came upon Marge hovering over the remains of what yesterday had been gloriously flowering hydrangea bushes and were now just butchered greenery.

"Look at them!" she cried, her arm jabbing in the direction of first one, then the other. "How could anyone *do* that?"

Gracie stood there, fists on her hips, staring down at them. "I don't know, but you're not the first one." As she slowly turned her head to look at her friend, she moved over to put an arm around Marge's waist. Her neighbor's appearance was almost as startling as that of her flowers: this woman was never seen by anyone when she wasn't looking her very best, but that was hardly the case now.

She had neither combed her hair nor applied makeup, and the robe she was wearing over her cotton nightgown was not a negligee, just a utilitarian, somewhat worn, flowered cotton one. *More like what I'd wear.*

"Is there any other damage that you know of, Marge?"

That must have been a new idea to the distraught woman, for she looked around almost fearfully. "I don't *think* so — but I'd better check." And she started across the grass.

Gracie walked beside her, ignoring the fact that her sneakers were, indeed, soaked before they neared the front corner of the house. Although the sun was already warm on her head and shoulders, she was conscious of her toes curling a bit from the cool dampness.

It was a relief to find no other evidence of any vandalism, and it was only then that Marge became aware of her own appearance. Her eyes grew wide with embarrassed concern as she gathered her robe closer around her. "I only hope no one saw me looking like this!"

Gracie grinned as she lightly punched her friend's shoulder. "Hey, they'll just think you're human, like the rest of us."

"I'll talk to you later, and you can explain then what you meant about me not being the first one." She disappeared through her back door.

Gracie's mind was racing with theories as this time she crossed back over the sopping grass of both yards and went into her own kitchen. Uncle Miltie was standing at the counter spreading peanut butter on a slice of bread. "Mornin', Gracie. Back from your walk already?"

She bent to remove her shoes before stepping off the throw rug. "I haven't gone yet. Gooseberry and I were over at Marge's to —"

"She's probably having a hissy fit about the electricity still being off."

"Actually, she didn't mention that."

"Really?" He was so surprised that he turned all the way around to face her. "I figured she'd be driven to distraction without a lighted mirror and a curling iron."

She couldn't help laughing, but sobered immediately. "Her other problem overshadowed that one. The blooms were removed from her hydrangeas during the night. And the worst of it is, she's the third victim."

His morning-whiskery jaw dropped a bit. "What do you mean?"

A nod. "It happened at the church and at Barb's."

"That's very strange — and also just a bit sinister."

"You're right." Barefooted, she started across the vinyl flooring. "But now I'm going to put on dry shoes and take myself and Gooseberry out for our walk."

"Well, keep an eye out for other butchered bushes! When it comes to flower felonies, I'm not sure whether the police will consider this culprit, whoever he is, to be a dangerous . . . stalker," he called after her.

She groaned at that pun, and, whistling for Gooseberry, headed out the front door.

Your world's so extra-beautiful this morning, Lord — washed clean by the rain and with crystal clear droplets clinging to each blade of grass and sparkling like diamonds. We did need the rain — Uncle Miltie said just yesterday that he'd have to water some of the flower beds today, which now isn't necessary.

But You know, God, about that other matter, those missing hydrangeas. Please help this to be nothing too serious — though it's getting harder to believe it's just a prank. Somehow, it seems too — specific.

If it IS the beginning of something really bad, I'd sure appreciate Your letting me or someone else know, so we can perhaps put a stop to it before any person gets hurt in any way. Whoever is doing this ugly thing needs You, too.

But then she came to an almost-stop herself, right there on the sidewalk. *Talk about Your answering prayers before they're even asked, God! Here I am, only a few steps away from the police station — and I hadn't even consciously thought of coming here.*

She often varied her route, so it was by chance (so she'd thought) that she'd happened to come this way today. She was not surprised that Gooseberry walked in right beside her and proceeded to check out the corners and the floor under the chairs as Gracie asked the woman at the desk, "Lucille, is Herb available? Could I speak with him for a few minutes?"

"I think so, Gracie." The clerk started to get up, then apparently changed her mind and waved her hand toward the short corridor. "He's always pleased to see you, so why don't you just go on back to his office?"

Gooseberry, who'd given no sign of paying attention to her since they'd arrived, was now, again, by her side as they went to the second room on the right. The tall, good-looking man glanced up as they got to the door, and was immediately on his feet to welcome her. "Gracie! It's always good to have you stop by — unless this is a professional call."

She knew that was a question, even though it wasn't inflected like that. "It may be, Herb — I honestly don't know at this point."

He was holding her hand, so it was easy to steer her toward one of the three armchairs in front of his desk. As he sat in the one next to hers, Herb Bower suggested, "Maybe we can figure that out together."

She relaxed back in her chair, at ease with this man she'd come to know quite well both at church and because they'd worked together — *well, sort of, anyway*, she thought — on a couple of strange happenings in Willow Bend. "I was at the church yesterday, checking on things I might need, since I'm now catering the Rotary dinner tomorrow. As I was leaving I noticed that someone had cut the flowers off those hydrangeas at the parking lot exit, but figured it was probably just some kids' prank or something.

"But Barb called later, and said someone had done that to *hers,* too. She was understandably upset about it, especially since she'd planned to take the very nicest of them to the fair tomorrow night."

A small frown creased his forehead, but he continued leaning back against the chair, elbows on its arms and fingers tented in front of him. She went on, "I hadn't heard of any vandalism to speak of taking place here in Willow Bend recently, so I still didn't think too much of the 'problem.' Barb, though, feared that, since this involved both our church and our organist/ choir director, it could be satanists or other weird folks with a grudge against the church.

"I tried to play down such a far-out possibility. But now, this morning, I found that the same thing happened to Marge, who, as you know, lives next door to me."

"Well, *that's* a relief!" He let out a long, slow breath. "I'm sure glad you stopped by to tell me about it."

"What?" *He must have misunderstood.*

"Four different properties have been hit thus far, Herb!"

He reached out to lay his hand firmly on her wrist. "That sounded callous, didn't it? And it's going to come across as even worse when I tell you there are now at least five. I also got word from Rick just a short time before you arrived, telling me that his mini-hydrangeas, those he calls his 'Pygmy Pee-gees,' had been cut off.

"You see, I've been hoping and praying ever since I learned about it that this wasn't some racial thing."

She blinked, startled, and her head cocked to the side. "Funny, I keep forget-ting that he's African American or that it means anything if he is."

"Of course you do, being *you* — and I'm pleased that there's been little evidence of racial prejudice here in Willow Bend. But let's face it, had he been the only person whose flowers were removed, we might have had to consider that possibility."

"Did he mention concern about that?"

"No, he didn't — nor did I. He seemed quite calm about it, actually. Said he just thought I should know."

Gooseberry was rubbing against her legs, leaving no doubt that he thought it time to get back to their interrupted walk. Gracie leaned over to rub his back and sides. "I guess that's my purpose for being here, too — just letting you know." She stood up and started for the door. "And now back to getting our exercise."

He walked her to the door. "I appreciate your coming, Gracie. I'm going to drive around to all these places and talk to the owners. And take pictures. At this point, I suspect it's just some kids acting up, but whether that's the case or not, it must be stopped."

"Yes." She nodded firmly. "It must."

Chapter Three

My mind's so full of hydrangeas that I'm now noticing them in many more yards than expected. Gracie didn't walk this part of town nearly as often as several other routes, though it was no farther away. Everything was neat and pleasant, and the plantings were every bit as attractive but, well, there wasn't as much variety of architecture. That was because these two-story and one-and-a-half-story dwellings for returning veterans had been built quickly and with little thought to variety in the years after World War II.

I'll have to mend my ways and include more parts of Willow Bend in my walking before I become a stranger to whole sections of this community in which I've spent most of my life.

None of the shrubs in this neighborhood appeared to have been mutilated — even though many were no farther away from sidewalks than Marge's. Could this fact give a clue that the culprit lived in her own part of town?

But no, the church was in a different section too, and Rick's, so none of the damaged yards were close together.

She crossed Main Street on the way home, within a half-block of the editorial offices of the *Mason County Gazette*, and decided on the spur of the moment to go in. Most of the paper's employees were busily working at their desks, and Sue Jameson, the features editor, looked up with a smile. "Good morning, Gracie. How are you doing?"

"Very well, thanks. And you?"

"Busy! Otherwise, I'm fine."

"In your business, I suspect that being busy is the condition of choice," Gracie replied, heading toward the glassed-in section, where sat Rocky Gravino. Her approach took longer than usual, since Gooseberry was basking in the attention and petting he was receiving from almost everyone he passed.

The editor-in-chief was working at his desk in shirtsleeves and with his collar unbuttoned. He finished going down over a column before glancing up — and instantly was on his feet, hands reaching for hers. "Hello, Gracie."

His slight frown of concentration had been replaced with an open-faced smile, and hers undoubtedly reflected her own pleasure at being with him. "I was on my way home from our morning walk, and thought I'd stop by."

He removed papers from the one chair other than his own. "Then have a seat — you've already had your exercise for the day."

She did as he'd invited. First they discussed the previous night's storm, and she told him her power was still off. With a little laugh, she commented, "Aren't we a pair? Especially since you're the ace newsman, who'd imagine we would spend the first minutes of my breaking into your busy day discussing the *weather?*"

He raised his shoulders in an exaggerated shrug. "If you don't tell, I won't either."

"Done!" Without further ado, she began to describe the peculiar hydrangea-mutilation situation. "Has anyone here heard about this? It seems inexplicable — if it's not some kids' prank."

"Nothing sounding anything like this has crossed my desk thus far." He reached to press something on his desk, and she could see Mike Struthers picking up his phone, then shaking his head as he heard Rocky out.

The upshot of the conversation was Rocky's, "How 'bout getting someone on this right away? We can still shuffle things around so a picture and the beginning of a write-up can be on page one."

Gracie was pleased at his determination to let people know about the plant attacks — and to give at least an implied appeal for help in catching the person or persons responsible.

He turned back to ask her, "Okay with you if they come around to your place and take pictures for a 'before' shot — you know, what all of these hydrangeas should look like?"

"Uncle Miltie will be ecstatic!" But then she had another idea. "But wouldn't it give your paper a better story if you'd have them shoot those of Molly Maginnis? She's the one who consistently wins at least several awards in this category at each year's fair."

"Great idea!" And he relayed the suggestion to Mike, along with the information that Gracie's flowers would be available in case Molly wasn't at home or — which seemed to Gracie most unlikely — refused to give her permission.

She had not asked if the *Gazette* office had lost its electricity the previous evening; if it had, at least it was on now, and this was encouraging. Hurrying home, however, she found her own section of town still without power.

She considered calling the power company to see if they had any idea as to when the power would be back. But she was glad she hadn't bothered when Marge phoned from her shop, where the power was on, to say she'd finally gotten through but had learned nothing more than "It shouldn't be long now."

Which did not sound overly encouraging to Gracie!

She found herself at loose ends. She'd expected to be doing things like cubing bread for the stuffing, but she didn't want to open the freezer even long enough to take out the loaves. And she didn't think she should open the refrigerator door to remove the eggs needed for making her special mayonnaise and the sweet-and-sour salad dressing — even if she hurriedly got these out, she'd again have to open the door to put them back, which would release even more cold air.

She called the church office, getting only the "canned" message requesting the caller to leave a message or call the parsonage. She chose the latter, only to hear Paul Meyer assure her that that end of town did have electricity. He also stated that the church's refrigerators were operational, as he'd taken a can of cold soda from there within the past hour.

When Gracie asked what he thought about the hydrangeas at the church's back door, he enthusiastically responded, "They're especially lovely this year. I'm grateful to you and Rick for having bought and planted them."

"You didn't notice them today —"

It wasn't meant as a question, but he answered that way — "I had to take things into the sanctuary, so I went in the front door. Then I worked in the office, but came back out the same way. Why did you ask?"

"Well-l-l, you won't think them pretty now, Paul. Someone's clipped off every single one of the fully blooming flowers."

"You're not serious!"

"I wouldn't joke about anything like this. But I do owe you an apology for not having notified you before now. I knew you were heading for the nursing homes, and then I forgot to call later. There have also been other losses — Barb and Marge and Rick have all been hit."

"Oh, no!" There was a brief pause before, "Has this been reported to the authorities?"

"Um-hmmm." And she told him how she had talked to both Herb and Rocky, and that there would be a story in the paper.

"The only problem with having the newspaper involved is that almost for sure this information will be on TV, too — and who knows?" he fretted. "Will we end up with a rash of copycat flower-cutters?"

"I sincerely hope not!" She almost told him that she had prayed what to do and then found herself in front of the police station. But somehow that seemed as though, in case things should turn out as he feared, Gracie might have been trying to cover her bases by putting any forthcoming blame on God — something she, of course, didn't intend.

"Do you think they'll want to photograph the plants here?" Paul asked.

"I don't know — but probably not, since Rocky mentioned getting permission from householders before taking pictures."

She next called Abe's Deli to ask if he happened to have any day-old bread for sale. Finding that he did, Gracie stopped there on her way to the church. "What's frustrating," she told him, "is that I keep lots of this in my big chest freezer in the basement."

"But you can't risk opening that," he agreed. He shook his head as she reached for the wallet in her purse. "This time the bread's on me." She started to protest, but he raised a hand, palm forward. "All of us appreciate your willingness to take on the catering on such short notice, Gracie, especially under these circumstances."

"But. . . ."

"No 'buts' about it, my friend! If you'd come in here moaning and groaning about the storm and the power outage, you might have been charged for that bread even if it *is* yesterday's. As it is, though, I really want to contribute my little bit."

It didn't feel right — yet she admitted to herself that she'd have done the same had their roles been reversed. And she wouldn't have wanted to make a big deal of it, either. Therefore, she merely said, "Thanks, Abe. It's really good of you."

"Well, I'm looking forward to enjoying it tomorrow night."

It was time for a change of subject. "Are you bringing anyone with you?"

He didn't look up from putting the loaves in two plastic bags. "Yes, I am this time. My sister, Sophie, is coming from Cleveland for the weekend, so she'll be with me."

"How nice! Will you be able to get free from here and have some quality time with her?"

He grinned. "Sophie's one of those on-the-go women, always wanting to be doing something constructive. She doesn't come often enough, but while she's here insists on helping with the baking — and she can always find something to scrub even when my cleaning service or I have already been over it." He sighed. "I wish she was able just to sit and visit, but there's no way that she won't be here with me, working in the delicatessen — whether I want her to or not."

"Is she about your age?"

"Two years older — and never lets me forget it! She should have married and had a dozen kids; as it is, she feels it's her motherly duty to oversee me and our younger brother."

"Pretty bossy, I take it?"

"Not quite, Gracie." But he was laughing. "Leave off the 'pretty' from your question, though, and you'll have it just right."

"And you brothers put up with it?"

He came around the counter to sit on the stool beside her. "It's love that makes her so difficult. That and her having promised Mom on her deathbed that she'd take care of us 'boys' — who were already in our thirties by then. *Most* of the time I can handle it, but Mike doesn't always do too well in that department."

"So she comes to visit you more often."

"And she is always welcome."

She was going out the door when she had

another thought, "You wouldn't have a dozen eggs you could spare, do you?"

"Probably." And he started for the big refrigerator. "Do you need them for anything in particular?"

"Well, I could stop at the market, or just buy commercial salad dressings. But I'd planned to make my own."

He reached in, brought out a carton, and handed it to her. "You're sure this is enough?"

"I'm sure."

But as she again started to reach into her purse, his hand covered hers. "I'm expecting a nice big piece of cherry pie for dessert tomorrow night!"

"It's a deal!" she assured him. *There's always pie left over, so I'll see to it he has a whole one to take home with him. Even if I have to combine leftover slices from several varieties!*

She'd resolved not even to look at the beheaded hydrangeas behind the church, but she couldn't keep herself from it. She was sure those flowers had been cut off with sharp shears — probably pruners, rather than a knife — which suggested to her that the destruction was not a spur-of-the-moment action.

She carefully kept on the macadam, on

the off-chance that any extra footprints might confuse the police when they came by. But she hadn't any other good sleuthing ideas, so she went on inside and directly to the kitchen.

She got out the extra-large cutting board that Uncle Miltie had made to use in the Eternal Hope kitchen, but before cubing even the first slices of bread, she decided first to prepare the cooked dressings. That way they'd have time to cool before being put into the refrigerator prior to her departure after finishing the morning's tasks.

She enjoyed working here by herself, and as she was cutting through stacks of bread, making the cubes, she found herself first humming, then singing next Sunday's anthem. It wasn't that she needed to — after all, they'd be having choir practice this evening — but she liked it. And it didn't matter right now that she was an alto and normally sang harmony: she just lowered the pitch a bit in order to handle the melody.

Oh, Lord, in love we come to Thee,
In faith, and hope, and charity,
We bring our happiness and pains,
We bring our losses and our gains.
Help us to learn, help us to grow
Closer to Thee — of Thee to know. . . .

These words are as simple and easy as those sung by the children in Sunday school, and the music's not at all difficult — but I like the un- affected old-fashionedness of both words and tune, and hope the congregation will.

Nobody came while she was there, not even Pastor Paul, which suited her fine. She liked being with people and was grateful for Uncle Miltie's living with her, but some- times it was good just to move around alone as she worked, carrying on a conversation with herself or with God — or singing.

Back home again, she went into the living room to ask, "What's your preference, Uncle Miltie: finding a restaurant that's open or opening a can of salmon or tuna to eat with unheated baked beans?"

"I'd enjoy salmon and beans, Gracie. Before coming here, I'd often have some- thing like that for a Sunday supper or for lunch. For that matter, those two cans would end up making me a couple of meals."

"I wish you'd tell me whenever you're hungry for something in particular."

His face became one big grin. "I think I just did, right?"

"Yes, you did." She knew her uncle well, and loved him the more for it. "And I'll look forward to having this meal again, even when our power's restored."

Gracie's old-fashioned can opener had got pushed back in the drawer, and, as she opened the cans, she was grateful it was no longer needed except in emergencies. *In spite of having cut myself so many times on these irregular, sharp edges, I'd almost forgotten how much more dangerous this can be since I switched to electric.*

He came to the kitchen as she was sliding the salmon out onto her smallest platter, and stopped her before the beans were dumped into a bowl. "If we're gonna make this like old times, Gracie, we can just spoon 'em right from the can onto our plates. That's what *I* used to do."

He was already taking his seat, so she presented him with the can and tablespoon with as much mock-seriousness as if it were a priceless crystal bowl. She didn't sit down, however, until after she'd filled their glasses with water from the faucet.

He reached for her hand and they bowed their heads for his prayer. "Dear Father, we thank You for this food, nutritious and plentiful — and *good,* too. We thank You for Your love and for Your watchful care over us again today.

"We also thank You for the rain, which

we really did need, and for there apparently being no *major* damage from the electrical storm. Please help those who are working around the clock to see that those of us without electricity will soon get it back — and give *special* care to those who are dependent upon it, like my friend, Al, in the nursing home, with all those tubes in him, and pumps running and everything. I know that they at least have generators and stuff, so please keep all those working properly, and help the staff to keep the patients from being too scared when they hear the reports of large areas of our town being without power.

"And, oh yes, God, I almost forgot to ask You to stop the person or persons who are cutting off all those pretty flowers. I don't know what their agenda is, but You do — and if there's anything Gracie and I can help with in putting an end to this, feel free to let us know what it is. Amen."

She opened her eyes and looked at him, almost expecting a grin or something at his having made that offer to God — but he was obviously serious. Well, she was, too, and she firmly echoed his "Amen."

They were nearly finished eating when Marge called to say, "I won't be going to choir practice tonight. I'm staying here at home, and I'm going to catch that person or those persons who are going around destroying people's property!"

"Do you think there's any real chance they'd come to your house again?"

"Well, they only took the ones by the sidewalk last night — which, of course, were the most outstanding. But I'll be ready for them if they try to get the ones by the porch steps!"

That sounded ominous, but Marge often spoke more emphatically than she acted and, to the best of Gracie's knowledge, she didn't own a gun. "What would you do?"

"I'd call the police, that's what I'd do. I've talked to Herb Bower — but he can be an overly conservative old fuddy-duddy, in case you didn't know that! He even made me promise to do nothing once I'd called the police."

"He does have a point, Marge." Gracie had experience of Herb's caution, as well as his sound professional instincts, and she knew Marge also respected him. But with her flowers at stake, she was bound to want action fast. "They are much better prepared for confrontations or emergencies than you are." And she added a hasty, "Or than I am."

"Well, anyway, I'm staying home tonight

and keeping a watch over things."

Gracie could make little headway toward changing her friend's mind, or her determination, so she finally hung up after warning, "Just don't trip over a throw rug or something while patrolling around in the dark!"

As it turned out, at choir practice, Marge was the only person missing, although Marybeth Bower was late because "Herb stayed on duty to help check out calls from people reporting that 'suspicious-looking people' had been seen at scattered sites throughout town.

"It's often like this," she explained. "There are many, especially older, people living alone, who take anything like this 'purloined posies' business very personally. Even if they have only roses or petunias or jacks-in-the-pulpit, they're sure the robbers — *always* more than one in their minds — will change whatever it is that they're stealing when they see how beautiful their flowers are."

Amy Cantrell seemed especially interested in what everyone was saying but didn't join the conversation. The attractive blond seventeen-year-old was without a doubt the best soprano in the choir — even if Estelle Livett disagreed. The older woman was overly conscious of her "professional training," meaning that she'd taken voice lessons over two decades earlier.

Barb didn't even want to talk about the damage to her own flowers, saying that was too painful. Rick, on the other hand, was downright indignant. "It's pretty darned unfair, blooms being taken from my mini-hydrangeas! I'd planned to take them to the fairgrounds tomorrow evening, so they'd be in Friday morning's judging. And I know I'm not the only one feeling that way.

"But it's outrageous that somebody's destroyed our church flowers. It's not just that Gracie and I bought them and planted them and fertilized them and tended them in every way we knew — but they were *God's* — and I don't take kindly to someone's stealing from Him!"

He looked at her and she nodded firmly, not adding anything. She was grateful for Barb's stating right then, "Time to begin practice, everyone — actually, *past* time."

There were a few groans when they learned that the practice was going to begin again with breathing exercises, then some scales, using the vowel-sounds preceded by an *m*, *ma-ma-ma-ma-ma-a-a*, *me-me-me-me-me-e-e*, *mi-mi-mi-mi-mi-i-i*, *mo-mo-mo-mo-mo-o-o*, *mu-mu-mu-mu-mu-u-u-u*, on each note going both upward, then back down, and, finally, in harmony.

One of the women grumbled when Barb started another exercise, and it was all Gracie could do to keep a straight face when Don Delano, the thirty-year-old chemistry teacher at the local high school with such a beautiful baritone voice, winked at her. He must have realized her amusement at Estelle's starting to defend Barb's methodology with a firm "It's very important to do these warm-up exercises — my voice professor quite insisted on it, you know, and it helped me tremendously!"

The "warm-up" seemed a lot longer than the six minutes indicated by Gracie's watch — and next they went over one or two verses of each of the hymns for the coming Sunday's congregational singing. They had to work on the last selection quite a bit, although it wasn't unfamiliar. Just a year ago the popular gospel singer, Cindy McGraw, had come out with a cassette on which she'd changed the timing near the end of the verse and also at two places in the chorus, adding a number of grace notes.

Tyne Anderson, who never seemed able to grasp the barest fundamentals of counting beats, was hopelessly lost because of these alterations, and her identical twin, Tish Ball, also unable to read music, couldn't figure out why the music continued on when she'd run out of printed words.

Since both sang alto, as Gracie did, she took it upon herself to sing more loudly than usual, hoping the twins would follow her lead.

Their anthem practice went remarkably well, so they had plenty of time to run through some other music they were scheduled to sing in upcoming weeks. One hymn was totally new and required the working-through of several especially difficult passages.

They had been seated thus far during the rehearsal, but now they stood to go through this week's anthem, "Closer to Thee," just one more time.

"Very good!" Paul Meyer, having been called out on a pastoral visit as he was eating dinner, had not arrived until they were working on their final number. "People will not only like the music, but will find it meaningful, helpful."

Gracie appreciated his words — and didn't believe he'd give such a compliment if he didn't mean it. But she understood that any good minister had to walk a very fine line when offering encouragement, being careful to speak the truth, and at the same time not to hurt parishioners' feelings.

I'm not sure I'd make a very good minister, God — and I'm glad You haven't asked that of me! I find it hard enough to do what I think I should and be what I think You want me to be, but to live in a fishbowl all the time, to have people watching me and talking about me and some maybe even hoping I'll make a mistake. No, thanks, God! I don't think I'm up to that!

Yet Elmo had spoken longingly about that very thing. He had on a number of occasions preached sermons, for example, on Laymen's Sundays or when their pastor was on vacation, and when Pastor Douglas had had that emergency surgery, and another time when Pastor Smith was laid up with pneumonia.

El had even talked about taking the two-year, in-depth, Saturday courses their denomination had begun to offer in order to help prepare people to become lay pastors. He dreamed of taking early retirement, then being able to help some struggling church that couldn't afford a college-and-seminary-trained minister.

She had not objected. And she thought that, had he lived, were they to have done this together, she, too, would have been very happy, as a pastor's wife.

Gracie deliberately turned her thoughts

to other topics when she realized that, with Elmo as her husband, she could have been happy if he'd been a carpenter or farmer or pharmacist or teacher or anything he had wanted to be.

Chapter Four

Both the men and women of the choir stayed long enough to help Gracie set up enough tables in the Family Activity Center, and she also accepted their offer to cover them with the table drapes. She assured them, however, that she and her helpers would be able to take care of the place settings.

She called home then, and Uncle Miltie answered almost immediately. "I'm sitting here at the kitchen table playing solitaire by the light of the kerosene lamp."

"In that case, I need not ask who's winning."

"It's not me tonight. I'm on my fourth try and still haven't successfully got rid of all my cards."

"Well, I'm ready to leave the church, and wondered if you'd like me to pick up a chocolate milk shake or something for you — if the Sweet Shoppe's got electricity."

"Sounds great. You getting one, too?"

"I'm hungry for a chocolate peanut-butter one this time."

"Oh." There was a slight pause as he considered possibilities. "Make it two of those, okay? It sounds too good to pass up, and we'll justify splurging on all those calories because we've become orphans of the storm, foodwise, at least."

She was laughing as she hung up the phone and walked out to the parking lot with Amy, Tish, and Tyne. All of them liked Uncle Miltie, and agreed that his excuse for indulging in something he enjoyed was as good as any they could come up with. Since she was driving Amy home, Gracie treated her to one of the delicious shakes, too, since she'd mentioned she'd never tried that flavor.

"Umm, it *is* good," Amy agreed, obviously enjoying the fact that every once in a while a small blob of peanut butter stopped the flow, necessitating the removal of the straw in order to suck vigorously from the other end.

"It makes me feel decadently childlike," Gracie confessed, managing to do as Amy had, even while driving. "I'd have loved one of these when I was seven!"

"Well, *I* like doing it now, at seventeen."

They talked about the girl's plan for college when she graduated. "What I'd really like is to go to a university where I could major in music education, while also getting the best voice training possible."

Gracie's drink was back in the car's plastic holder, so she could reach over to squeeze Amy's arm. "I sincerely hope you will, dear. You have a lovely voice, and who knows where that can take you?"

"I — don't tell most people, but my dream for years has been to study opera, so I suppose I should go to New York City."

"I know your parents will support you."

"It's — largely a matter of money, as you know."

Yes, I do know — all too well. Gracie had learned about that after her involvement with getting Amy back when she'd been abducted. Since then, Amy had come to be almost like the daughter she'd never had. "Your lead role in that community theater production of *The King and I* was truly remarkable, Amy. And so were your parts in all the school performances. And you know how we cherish you in our choir.

"It seems to me that videos of those just might help you get scholarships to the school of your choice. At least it's worth a try."

Uncle Miltie's cards were still on the table, but Marge was now with him as

Gracie entered the kitchen. "Am I glad you're back, Gracie!" her neighbor cried. "I've been so frightened!"

She looked every bit as disturbed as she sounded. "What happened?" Gracie demanded.

"Well, I was wearing these dark clothes and was outside, hiding in the bushes, for a long time. But then I went back inside, finally. It was just too uncomfortable — and scary!

"Everything was quiet for awhile, then Charlotte started barking, and I heard noises outside. I'm *sure* someone was there, out back — but I couldn't see anyone. Or anything. But Charlotte kept on barking!"

There's nothing unusual about that Shih Tzu of yours making a rumpus — especially since she'd sense how high-strung you are right now! But such a comment was uncalled for. "It's just as well that you came to be with us." *Definitely so for your peace of mind.*

Gracie changed the subject by asking if they'd enjoy one game of Scrabble. But she couldn't feel too triumphant when she won, since she knew the others were unable to keep their minds off of what Uncle Miltie referred to as their "hydrangea mystery."

Marge still made no move to go home, so Gracie asked if she'd like to stay. "I shouldn't — and Charlotte doesn't ever stay alone at home overnight."

Realizing that her uncle was frowning and about to say something, Gracie responded quickly, "She's been with us a number of times, like when you went to those trade shows and when you were in the hospital for gall bladder surgery. And she and Gooseberry get along very well, as you know."

It took no further coaxing for Marge to agree. Using a powerful flashlight, Gracie went with her — on the sidewalk this time instead of crossing their yards — to pick up the necessaries: nightgown, face cream, toothbrush, and Charlotte, along with one of her favorite toys.

Neither of them mentioned checking on the hydrangeas.

It wasn't long before Marge was settled in one of the spare bedrooms always kept in readiness for visits from Gracie's son and his family, or her niece, Carter.

Gooseberry gave his own welcome to the little dog. They had, after all, once endured a traumatic ordeal together. After a few minutes of sniffing and rubbing each other, they curled up and went to sleep. Marge stood there shaking her head. "You're sure that Gooseberry of yours isn't a dog?"

"The way those two get along does make

one wonder," Uncle Miltie admitted dryly. "But you know the vet keeps insisting he's a cat. It must be that they survived that same poisoning!"

He made his goodnights right after that. Then Gracie, stating that she, too, was bushed and planned to follow his example, started to get ready for bed as soon as their guest went upstairs.

She had just finished brushing her teeth when the phone rang. Gracie glared at the noisemaker as she walked across the kitchen floor, but was grateful she'd tried not to sound out of sorts when hearing, "*Hi,* Mom. I hope this isn't too late to be calling."

"It's *never* too late for you to call, Arlen." She pulled one of the kitchen chairs closer and sat down. "How *are* you and the family?"

"Great, actually — though a little lonely. With your grandkid off at church camp, this place seems almost too quiet."

She could mentally picture her brown-hair-and-eyed 8-year-old grandson, who not only was named for Elmo, but resembled him a lot. "Wow, it doesn't seem like he's old enough for that already!"

He laughed. "Don't tell El that — he thinks he's practically a man, going off like

74

this for his first time away from us."

"He *has* stayed with me," she reminded. "When you and Maddie had that conference in Chicago two years ago, he and I had a great time together."

"Indeed you did — but you're part of the family."

She sighed. ". . . Even if we don't get together as often as I'd like."

"Come any time you like, Mom. The door's always open and we'd love to have you — as though you didn't know that already."

"Yes, I do know that, just as you know that's true of my house and town — and my heart."

"That's one reason for calling. Is it okay if the three of us come for a few days? I've been telling El about the County Fair and everything, and we're thinking of perhaps being there from Sunday through Thursday, if that would suit you."

"If that would suit me?" she repeated. "It most certainly will, dear! Come as soon as you can and stay as long as you're able."

"Is my cousin going to be with you?"

He obviously recalled how her niece Carter always enjoyed this, too, and often came from Chicago for at least a day or two at the fair. "Carter said she was aiming for

Saturday — but I'll bet she'll stay over if she knows you'll be here."

"Great!" But then he changed the conversation to, "So what have you got involved with that's new or different or mysterious in Willow Bend?"

He often teased about her part in having helped solve a couple of cases, so she was a bit on the defensive. "It's not that I *try* to get involved, Arlen. . . ."

"If I'm not mistaken, Mom, I believe that verb to be in the present tense. Is something happening again *now?*"

"Probably not." She was determined to keep her voice light and manner breezy. "It's just that someone stole those beautiful hydrangeas from the rear entrance to our church, and those from a couple of the church members, too — but I guess that's all."

"You're concerned about this?"

"Wouldn't *you* be? A number of us have put a lot of planning and work into these, and were hoping for some ribbons at the fair!"

"Maybe you'll still win some."

"Hoping doesn't do too much good when we're missing the flowers themselves."

"That's true." He sighed, then said more cheerfully, "Well, I'm not going to lose too much sleep over this situation, since you can't get in too much trouble or danger over just a bunch of flowers. Right?"

She chuckled. "It doesn't seem too likely, does it?"

"But just in case," he persisted, "I'm gonna ask you to promise to stay out of trouble this time."

She considered that a safe promise to make, at least with one qualifying word. "Sure, I promise to try."

"You do realize that I recognize the difference in wording between my question and your answer?"

"Well, how *can* I make such a commitment, Arlen? You don't want me to lie to you, do you?" She successfully switched the subject to her "getting roped into the Rotary Club dinner," which he said didn't surprise him, for if there was ever a person who couldn't say, "No," it was she.

They then spoke of things with which he was involved, and some remembered fairs and parades of his youth. No, he had not played his French horn for years — not since those long-ago high school days — and he was going to hang up now before he got too nostalgic. . . .

Morning dawned, bright, crisp and beautiful, and Gracie was ready for it. She got up even before the alarm went off, and took her shower. It was light enough that she had not thought to press the electric switch near the door. But still there was no electricity when she remembered to try after toweling.

Hoping against hope that the problem might just be a blown fuse, she headed for the kitchen — but there was still no power available there, either.

This is getting annoying, God — and not just for me, although it does, of course, make things a lot more difficult because of the dinner tonight. But I know that with Your help we can do whatever has to be done.

There are, however, a great many folks who are having a lot of trouble dealing with an emergency that lasts this long!

She felt a bit guilty about grumbling, and admitted to herself — then to God — that she had no business trying to tell Him how to do those things He'd been taking care of so well throughout the ages. *I apologize, Father. Somehow I just seem to be in the habit of trying to take control, but I'll work harder to see the bigger picture of how or where I fit into Your plans.*

Gracie still thought it was best not to open the refrigerator door, but, "If we still don't have electricity by noon, Uncle Miltie, I'll try to find some dry ice to tide us over a bit more." In the meantime, there were three only slightly overripe bananas on the counter, one of which he decided to use sliced on his granola cereal, along with powdered milk stirred into cold tap water.

Gracie waited for his verdict before joining him in downing the same thing. Both pronounced it to be every bit as good as using milk from a carton. Marge, however, turned up her nose and wouldn't even accept a banana. She was going to check out her house and would pick up some toaster-pastries while there, and would eat those as soon as the coffee finished perking at her store.

The morning paper arrived as she was preparing to leave. Gracie had not expected to read it right away, but then she glanced at the front page. "Marge! Miltie! Look at this!"

He hurried as quickly as possible with his walker, and Marge came to her other side, exclaiming, "I can hardly believe this! Molly Maginnis in living color on page one!"

"Along with those magnificent hydrangeas of hers!" Gracie added.

The banner headline read, "WILLOW BEND VICTIMIZED BY FLOWER BANDIT," and there were shots of the vandalized hydrangea plants belonging to Rick and Barb, as well. The accompanying story described the attacks on the plants, mentioning that the Eternal Hope Community Church had also suffered from missing blooms.

But what was the most amazing part to those standing in Gracie's kitchen was that the other story, running over onto page eight, had a picture of Molly with her dramatic wall display of all the blue ribbons her flowers had won during the past years! Under one of her pictures was the quote, "I'll, of course, be showing my hydrangeas at the fair again, for they're especially lovely this year. But my heart goes out to those poor people who've lost those flowers they may have planned to enter."

There was one paragraph towards the first story's end in which the possibility of a connection between the attacks was mentioned. And the readers were reminded that all flowers and other items to be judged at the County Fair would have to be taken to the fairgrounds tonight.

And that led to a closing request that any information or even suspicions pertaining to the crime at hand be given to the police as soon as possible.

"One thing's for sure," Uncle Miltie

stated, heading for the other room, "I'm keeping my distance from that woman for the next couple of weeks, maybe months! She's always been puffed-up about that green thumb of hers, and this is going to make her insufferable!"

That was probably true, but Gracie suggested, "I guess she comes by it naturally. It was her grandmother, along with several other women, who started the Willow Bend Flower Club way back when Mrs. Hartzell was the president of it right up till she died, then Molly took her place."

"So how big a group is it now?" he asked. "How come I've never heard of it?"

She cocked her head, thinking. "Now that you mention it, Uncle Miltie, I haven't either, for a while. And," she glanced again at the write-up, "I saw no reference to it here."

Marge was near the doorway through which she and Charlotte were about to leave. "I, for one, wouldn't choose to be in any organization headed by her!"

"You know, she hasn't always been quite this difficult." Gracie was making an effort to be fair. "Something seemed to happen to her personality a few years back, when that husband of hers ran out on her." And then she regretted having worded it that way, for

Marge's own husband had divorced her in order to marry a much younger woman.

Thank goodness her friend apparently didn't take exception to that, for she said, "That was a surprise — to everyone, not just her. I'd suspected things weren't going smoothly between them, for there was a lot of bickering even in public. But I liked Frank and was surprised when he took off like that, with just a note to her — something about his 'needing space,' or 'having to find himself.' "

As she left, Uncle Miltie declared, "Hunh! I'd sure need to 'have space' or 'find myself' were I married to Molly." He punctuated that remark by forcefully setting down the rear part of his walker with each step he took toward the living room.

Gracie was putting their dishes and silverware into the sink as Marge came running back in. "Gracie! It's *your* flowers now, too — those deep pink ones!"

They filed silently out to regard the damage. Every single one of her hydrangeas that were almost or completely open had vanished. Gracie stood there, hand over her abdomen. "I — feel almost sick at my stomach — *violated.*"

"Those dirty . . . !" But Uncle Miltie didn't finish that exclamation as he glared down at these plants, which had given him and Gracie such pleasure.

She turned on her heel and headed for the house. "I reported those others, and I'd better call Herb about this, too!"

The phone was picked up on the first ring. "Willow Bend Police — Chief Bower speaking."

"Oh, Herb, they got *my* hydrangeas now, too."

"Gracie? Is that you?"

"I'm sorry, I should have said so — but Herb, we just discovered that our flowers were taken, too!"

"During the night?"

"It had to be — I looked at them just before dark." And then she remembered to tell him about Marge's staying overnight. "She was especially frightened because her dog Charlotte barked so much, probably because of someone doing something in my yard, not hers."

"Is it the same MO — same *modus operandi?*"

"Exactly the same! They were cut off with well-sharpened shears, not a knife — and every single one of them was carried away, not just thrown down on the ground."

"If that's the case, is there any point in my coming over?"

It had not occurred to her that he wouldn't. "Well-l-l, I suppose it's not really necessary. . . ."

"On second thought, I think I will. I'll be there within a couple of minutes."

She supposed he'd recognized her need to have him turn up, if only to make her feel as if something was being done. "I'd appreciate that, I really would."

Her mind was roiling, and she kept trying to work out a possible reason for what was happening. She couldn't be sure that it was a coincidence that it was all taking place as the annual County Fair exhibition was getting underway. Could somebody have planned it for then to hide some other reason?

She was back outside again by the time Herb arrived. As expected, there were no more helpful clues in her yard than at the other sites. He did, however, take several pictures — something Gracie had refrained from doing. "Don't show them to me, Herb. I don't wish to see this damage ever again."

He placed a hand on her shoulder. "I'm sorry, Gracie. I've seen how beautiful they were, and I know how sad this makes you."

"It's become more than just a troublesome, miserable concern — it's a genuine first-class worry. For someone to be so rotten, so self-centered, so-whatever-the-reason-might-be as to take away decent, law-abiding individuals' attempts at helping God create something beautiful is not only dastardly, but *cruel*. Perhaps even crazy?"

Before he had the chance to respond, she went on with, "And who knows what this perpetrator might do next?"

They discussed the possibility of its being just a prank, but they could come to no conclusion as to why anyone should be picking on these specific people. It's true they were all members of the choir of the Eternal Hope Community Church, and that flowers also had been taken from there, but no matter how one looked at it, it didn't make sense.

And then there was Gooseberry, who seemed to be acting a bit strange — though Gracie would be the first to admit he was hardly the most typical cat in the world. He'd been accustomed to lying under the pink hydrangeas for hours, but now he seemed to be avoiding it, giving it a wide berth and not nosing around there while the humans were checking it out. Curiosity, after all, had never killed this cat!

He was also sticking closer to Charlotte,

Marge's dog, than to anyone other than Gracie.

She knew Herb should get back to his office so, stifling her sense of unease as best she could, Gracie thanked him for coming. "And now I must be off to the church to get things underway for tonight's dinner."

"I'm looking forward to that, and so is Marybeth."

He probably said that to make me feel better. "Who's watching the kids?"

"Amy said she would, and they're delighted. She's their favorite sitter."

She walked to his car with him, but before she got back to the house she had to respond to the cell phone in her pocket.

"Hi, Gracie, this is Molly."

Oh, no! I didn't need this right now. But she tried to keep her voice free of annoyance, "Hello, Molly, how are you?"

"Splendid, I have to say. Did you see the paper this morning?"

"Yes, I did. That was a very nice article, and the pictures are excellent."

"They are, aren't they?"

Her voice was not only cheerful but practically euphoric — not the usual condition for a woman who never even seemed contented, much less happy. At the moment, Gracie wasn't feeling that great herself, so she said nothing.

"This has been a good year for most plants — enough rain at the times it was needed, nights not too cold nor days too terribly hot."

"That's right, Molly. We haven't had to water anything so far — haven't even got the hoses out, for that matter."

"Yes." There was a moment's silence before, "Well, I must get busy. Other tasks call, you know."

"Take care and have a nice day," Gracie told her, almost automatically.

"Oh, I'm sure I will. But it will be a busy one, too, what with everything that needs to be done."

Yes, I suppose it will, Gracie thought. *You'll be working at cutting your very nicest hydrangeas and putting them in your very prettiest vases and taking them to the fair.* But Gracie didn't like her own attitude right now, so she determined to make more of an effort to be pleasant, "I hadn't realized you'd won that many ribbons so far. You do have a way with flowers, Molly."

"Some of us just have a green thumb, you might say. My family has been passing it down for several generations now. It's something to take pride in, don't you think?"

Several more minutes passed, with Gracie sure Molly needed no answer and provoked at herself for letting the woman go on talking for so long. She waited through several more self-satisfied comments, then rather impatiently got in the words, "Thanks for calling, Molly, but I, too, have something which must be done right away."

"Oh, but let me tell you just one more thing."

"I can't, Molly, I really must leave this minute. We can talk later. 'Bye for now." And she disconnected the call. *Phew! I wasn't sure I was ever getting away from her! But, even so, I hope she doesn't consider that too rude.*

The phone rang again as she was putting things in her ten-year-old, dark blue Cadillac, but she decided to ignore it. *You see, Fannie Mae,* addressing the beloved automobile, which seemed to her much more than just a means of conveyance, *it's almost surely Molly calling back. But even if it's not, I must get to the church. The others are probably there by now.*

At least she hoped they were!

Chapter Five

Gracie went directly to the church, finding only one of her two helpers already there. Tish Ball had not yet arrived an hour later — which did surprise her, for this woman was one of the most dependable persons in all of Willow Bend and points beyond.

Gracie went to the phone in the hallway and tried to reach Tish, then even called the other Turner twin. "Tyne, this is Gracie. I'm sorry to bother you, but do you know where your sister is? She was supposed to meet me here at the Family Activity Center over an hour ago, to help get everything ready for the dinner tonight."

"I'm sure she didn't forget it, Gracie," she said. "Tish even mentioned that to me this morning — she was looking forward to it. I wouldn't worry about it if I were you. She's probably just running a bit late."

Time passed quickly there in the church kitchen. Eleanor McIver was a good ten years older than Gracie, but even on her way to being an octogenarian, Eleanor was as active and cheerful as ever. She was also one of the leading lights of the Willow Bend Volunteer Firemen's Auxiliary, heading up most of their frequent money-making dinners, wedding receptions, and other catered events.

Preparations were going so well that by ten o'clock Gracie realized that she and Eleanor should be able to handle everything on their own. But she was getting more and more concerned about Tish. Again going to the hall phone, she called home. "Hi, how are things there?"

"Undeniably perfect — not one single phone call since you left," her uncle reassured.

She laughed. "You still consider these work, don't you?"

"Well-l-l, I like making calls — when absolutely necessary or 'cause I love the person — but you must admit that most of those coming in here I can do without." He cleared his throat. "So, Gracie, how about letting me know why you called me?"

He, too, sounded worried when she mentioned her concerns and said she'd hoped Tish might have got in touch. "I phoned Tyne earlier, and hate having to bother her again."

"How about John? Her husband might know something."

"I thought of that, but decided to check with you first. You'll let me know if you hear anything, won't you?"

"You know I will!"

She checked the number for Harry Durant's garage and gas station, where Tish's husband worked. "He's under a truck right now," she was told, when she called there.

"Will he be there long?"

"I doubt it — he's been working on it quite awhile."

"Might you have a cordless phone or something? Would it be possible for me to talk with him for just a minute?"

There was a brief silence which she quickly filled with, "This is Grace Parks, and I need to ask a question."

"Could I pass it on for you?"

She didn't recognize the voice, but it wasn't Harry, so it probably was one of the other mechanics. "I'd prefer speaking with him directly, if that's possible."

"Okay, I'll see what I can do."

She heard a shouted, "Hey, John, there's a woman on the phone, a Ms. Parks. She says she's gotta talk to you." There were various background sounds, which may be why she didn't hear a reply. Then she was told, "Just a minute."

Next a familiar voice was saying, "Good morning, Gracie."

She certainly hoped it was! "I'm sorry to bother you at work, John, but I'm concerned, and decided I'd better check with you. Tish was planning to help Eleanor McIver and me here at the church today, but she hasn't shown up."

"She mentioned it at breakfast, so I know she didn't forget. She probably stopped off at Tyne's on the way. You know the two of them!"

"But I've already called Tyne, and they'd talked on the phone a couple of hours ago, and everything was apparently okay. Is it possible she might have had car trouble or something?" Hoping he'd not interpret that as an aspersion cast on the maintenance and care he'd give his wife's vehicle, she quickly added, "Does she carry a cell phone?"

"Usually — though she sometimes forgets. Tell you what, Gracie, I'm gonna hang up here and try to get hold of her that way."

"Good idea! And let me know right away, okay?" In the meantime she'd pray that he'd quickly reach Tish — and that she was all right.

"Sure, Gracie. I'll call right back — oh, how about giving me the church's number?"

But only a few minutes later she received word that John had been unable to reach his wife either in her car or at home. "I've got to get back to finishing this truck, since it's a rush job, but I'll try her again in another fifteen or twenty minutes. But don't fret about it, she's probably just stopped at a store or something."

"Maybe so." But she didn't believe it — that wasn't the Tish she knew, the one who knocked herself out trying to be helpful, the one who was always on time.

Would it be okay for me to call Herb, God? If there's been an accident or anything, he'd surely have reports — yet, if he did get anything like that he'd certainly have contacted her husband straightaway.

She should probably wait for John to call her again with further news, but she felt apprehensive enough to make an excuse to leave Eleanor at work in the kitchen and sneak away to use her own cell phone to contact the police station. Luckily, she was put through right away. "I have a question, Herb, but it's not meant to be nosy or anything."

"Whatever it is, it's okay, Gracie."

"What's okay?" She couldn't help sounding jumpy, it seemed.

"You don't have to give a preamble. Just

calm down and ask your question. You know I trust you."

"Oh." In a way it was harder just to jump right in like this. What if she came across as stupid or unstable in having fears about someone missing — or *delayed* — only a few hours?

"Well, Tish Ball was supposed to be helping here at the church today, but she hasn't shown up. I've called both her sister and her husband, but they don't know where she is — and since she's not answering at home or from her car, I'm calling to make sure she hasn't been involved in an accident."

"Slow down, Gracie." His voice remained steady and soothing. "I've seen or heard nothing that could account for her not being where she's supposed to be. So she probably just forgot, and went somewhere else."

"That would sound reasonable, except that she's the one who brought up the subject to both John and Tyne this morning. So we're sure she *did* remember."

"Well, something could have come up unexpectedly, and she wasn't able to get you right away, and then forgot."

"She's not like that, and you know it!"

"Everyone sometimes does atypical things. She's human, you know."

"Yeah, I do know that," she admitted with a sigh. "It's just that I have this uneasy feeling that something's very wrong concerning her — and that I should be doing something about it."

"Like — what?"

He sounded a tad alarmed, so she hastened to reassure him. "Oh, nothing big, nothing dramatic or anything."

"Gracie?"

Was there a quality of appeal in the way he said her name? "What?"

"How about waiting a little longer — you know, give her a chance to get there?"

She had to respond to that, "It's already been a couple of hours, Herb."

"But she might come in a few more minutes."

And she might not! "Well, I'll wait a few more minutes if that will make you happy."

"Then what?"

There's that suspicious quality in your voice again! "We'll see, Herb. We'll see. . . ."

"Gracie? What are you planning to do then, Gracie?"

"Oh, try making some more calls — stuff like that." *I'm not about to limit myself any more than that, Herb Bower, whether you like it or not!*

★ ★ ★

When the "few" minutes she'd promised had multiplied to ten, she slipped off her bibbed apron, folded it neatly and laid it on the counter. "We've done really well here, Eleanor. As you know, this," touching the yellow tablet on the counter, "is the fairly complete timetable I've set up estimating by what point we should have accomplished various tasks. So far, even with just the two of us, we're ahead of schedule.

"So I'm going to run a few errands. I expect to be back shortly, but if I *should* be delayed, don't let that bother you. Just go on with the next item."

"No problem," Eleanor assured. "Using mini-carrots instead of cutting up big ones, and having the salad dressings ready and the bread cubed and onions and celery already diced for the stuffing, I'd say we're in excellent shape. I'll see you when you get back, so don't worry."

Eleanor and Ben had raised their six sons on their dairy farm, seen them all through college, and were still doing most of the chores themselves. Now, after telling Gracie to take her time, she kept on working.

Gracie, on the other hand, was feeling pressure — though not from the food preparation. Where *was* Tish? Well, first of all, she'd go to the Ball home to check if she and her car were there — that she hadn't fallen and broken a leg or something.

You know, Elmo, if either of us was missing, I'm sure everyone would be out there beating the bushes, or at least insisting that the police start investigating.

I don't think I'm more suspicious than average, even though I've been involved with a couple of cases with Herb. But it does seem to me that if a situation appears this atypical, then either I'm not understanding the particular situation or something's actually going on that's not normal at all.

She drove slowly down the block as she approached the bright yellow house on the corner of Seventh and Cedar streets. The lawn was freshly mowed, the outside neat and trim, as always. The garage door was closed, so she couldn't tell if a vehicle was inside, but there wasn't one out front. Through the screen door, however, it looked as if the wooden door behind it was standing open, though she couldn't tell for sure.

Pulling to the curb, she turned off the engine and tucked the keys inside her pocket. What with leaving the church in a hurry, she'd neglected to pick up her purse

— an oversight she seldom made. Oh, well, she'd never had an accident, and there was plenty of gas in the tank, so she wasn't going to worry about it.

Nobody came when she rang the doorbell, so Gracie tried again, then called through the screen. Next, even knowing she shouldn't do so, legally speaking, she stepped inside. After all, she and Tish had known one another forever. "Tish," she called, then repeated it much more loudly, "*Tish*, are you here?"

The only sounds were the bubbling of air in the large, rectangular fish tank and the ticking of the tall, walnut grandfather clock in the corner of the living room. Shouting Tish's name again, she walked into the dining room, kitchen, and even the bathroom, in case she might have fallen and was lying somewhere, unconscious.

She went up the stairs and entered each of the three bedrooms and bath before going back down. *Now what, Gracie Lynn Parks?* she demanded of herself. *First of all, anyone seeing you come into the house as you did, and staying as long as you are, will assume you're up to no good.*

Deciding to ignore that possibility, she went to the phone to call the service station again. John must have been standing near the phone, for he was speaking into it almost at once. "I tried calling you a little bit ago, Gracie, but you weren't at the church."

That sounded accusatory, as though she hadn't kept her part of the bargain. But she ignored the nuance, suspecting he was merely upset. "How did you make out, John? Did you talk with Tish?"

"No, I didn't. I wasn't able to get hold of her."

"I haven't either, and I'm in your house right now. . . ."

"*My* house?" he repeated. "What are you doing *there?*"

"Well, I'm still worried about her, so decided to come over to see if she might have fallen down the steps or — or something. But she's not here."

"You're *sure* she's not around?"

"The doors were standing open, but she didn't come when I rang the bell and called. So I came inside and checked both upstairs and down." She remembered that she'd missed something, though. "I didn't go to the basement, though — hold on a minute and I'll run down."

She thought he was saying something as she put down the phone, but she didn't want *not* to look there in case that's what he was about to tell her. Everything proved to be in good order there, also. She was a little breathless from running back up the basement steps to report, "It all seems fine down there, as well."

"Of course it is."

"Look, do you have any idea where she could be?"

"I told you, she probably just went shopping or something, and somehow forgot about meeting you at the church."

He was starting to sound annoyed, and she couldn't really blame him. But she had to ask, "Would she be driving the white Ford?"

"Yes." Another sigh. "I've got the pickup."

"Well, there's no vehicle outside, but I'll check through the garage window. I'm leaving right away. Should I lock the doors — or do you always leave them open like this?"

"We never leave them open. Well," he went on reluctantly, "she must have forgotten to lock them today — but we usually do."

"Do I just push in that little button on each lock, and pull the doors shut? Will that be enough?"

His even louder exhalation indicated agitation. "Yes, that's what we do!"

"Okay, John. And thanks."

I guess this isn't the wisest thing I've ever done, but. . . . She'd been standing there looking around while talking, but as she replaced the receiver she noticed seven numbers written on a pad beside the phone, obviously a phone number.

But what focused her attention was the name jotted next to the number.

Oh, dear! I didn't expect this!

She decided to check back with Uncle Miltie again before leaving, but didn't consider it necessary to tell him she wasn't at the church. He could report no call from Tish, but commented, "You know, Gracie, I've been thinking about that little walk I took this morning, after you left."

He didn't often walk with her, insisting he didn't want to hold her back, but did occasionally go around several blocks, perhaps just to make sure he still could. She'd assured him over and over that she didn't mind sometimes going slower, but he was stubborn about some things. "Where did you go?"

"Out Maple for two blocks, then up Fifth Street. What I was just remembering was that as I was coming toward Molly Maginnis's house — I planned to stop and rest there on her wall, you know — I saw one of the Turner twins going in there.

"I don't know which it was, though, 'cause I can't tell them apart even when they're together. But since no car was parked along the street there, I assumed it was Tyne, seeing as how she lives fairly close."

She sucked in her breath sharply, but made herself speak as normally as possible. "Was Molly there to greet her?"

"Um-hm. She was holding the screen door open. Nothing seemed unusual."

"And Tish — or whichever — went inside?"

"Yep, she did." But then he backpedaled a little, "Not that there couldn't be an excellent reason for her being there, mind you."

"Oh, I realize that." *But what am I going to do about it?* "Well, I'd better hang up and get busy."

He'll think I'm busy getting ready for that dinner — and goodness knows I should be! But there's that phone number of Molly's on Tish's pad and Uncle Miltie's seeing one of the twins going in there.

She shook her head briskly, as if to force unruly thoughts into line.

Gracie got back into her car and drove to the other house. Tish's car was not parked along the street, so Gracie figured her friend must have walked over — or had left already. Hurrying up the walk and figuring there might still not be electricity — she'd forgotten to ask her uncle if it was back on yet at home — she knocked on the door.

At the same time, she heard what sounded like an automatic garage door being raised. She hesitated for only a moment before running around the house. As she got to the corner, she saw that Molly's big Chrysler had just emerged and was turning into the short bit of alley, then made a left out onto Main Street!

She tried to get the driver's — Molly's — attention by waving her arms and calling, but she didn't succeed. *And the worst part of this is that I think I saw something or someone on the backseat, all wrapped up in a blanket!*

It couldn't be Tish, could it? She had no real reason to suspect that, but . . . *Oh, God, was that Tish?* She felt she had a right to ask. *Did You bring me here at this time so I'd see that car leave — with whatever it was in the back? If You did arrange for that, then You must mean for me to follow, don't You?*

I don't understand any of this! I simply have no idea why or what's going on!

And Molly's car was getting away!

Turning, Gracie started to run back the

way she'd come. Even as she made haste, she couldn't help noticing the interior of Molly's glassed-in sunroom-addition, which had been built at the same time the new garage was constructed at the other side of the house.

With floor-to-ceiling glass all across the back and toward the east, it was bright and cheerful. Her gaze was now riveted not by the room itself, but by what it contained. There were flowers and plants covering every stand and chair and massed on the closed top of the baby grand piano. There were whole flats of tiny to small plants, but what couldn't be missed was the almost sur-real display of flowers — every single one a hydrangea!

They were in all kinds and varieties of containers — vases, bottles, bowls, and pans — and large quantities filled buckets and tubs! Some were white, but most were in every shade from palest pink through almost-red, and from a very light blue through deeper shades, a few almost indigo.

Wow! Gracie thought, impressed, despite herself. *Compared with the limited number for sale at nurseries and in catalogues, plant developers would love to see all of these.*

And the contest judges at the fair can't help but feel the same way!

But she wouldn't dwell on that, for she must concentrate on the business at hand — following Molly's car! She was racing against time, and it didn't matter what any neighbors or passersby might think as she took off in pursuit.

She was parked in the right direction to scoot down the nearest alley and onto the street Molly had taken. There weren't that many traffic lights in the whole town, but there were numerous stop signs in residential neighborhoods, mostly to slow down speeders. Molly, obviously still obeying traffic laws, was only three blocks ahead.

Oh, Lord, help me keep her in sight without her becoming conscious of being tailed. If only I'd picked up my purse at the church and brought it with me!

But she didn't have her cell phone with her now and that was that. She couldn't take the time to stop somewhere to call Herb Bower, to let him know what was going on, or what she was doing. Still, she supposed that was just as well, since he'd try to talk her out of trailing Molly.

I do wonder where we're heading — and why. Molly's been driving at exactly thirty-five miles per hour through town, but is now raising that to precisely forty-five. She knows there's that sign along the road indicating the new maximum. Is this a conscious effort on her part not to call attention to herself — to make sure no one, certainly no policeman, has any reason to stop her?

And then her speed jumped again, as soon as it was legal, not fluctuating more than a few miles per hour as they sped through the next five miles of farmland.

There were trees up ahead, and Gracie suspected where they were heading — a destination she almost feared under this circumstance. Elmo used to enjoy outings with Frank Maginnis to their neighbor's hunting cabin located on a secluded part of wooded acreage he owned just on this side of the county line.

Frank had told Elmo about Molly's being angry when he'd insisted on holding on to this portion of his ancestral farm while selling off the rest at a fabulous price. Elmo also shared with Gracie — but only after Frank had departed Willow Bend so unexpectedly — that he thought this hideaway, which Molly hated, may have been the main thing which had caused his friend to stay around as long as he had.

Frank and Molly had no children, and their relationship had apparently been rocky for years, although no one had suspected how troubled their marriage was. At least, not until later, when looking back. Gracie and Elmo certainly hadn't heard or contributed to any gossip about the Maginnises, but she wondered again why Frank hadn't just got a divorce and left, instead of exiting in the middle of the night — and losing everything.

Those woods were now along the right side of the road, and Molly was slowing — turning off onto the rutted gravel road on which Gracie had only rarely traveled.

It's strange. I've been concentrating so much on all these other things that I've avoided considering what to do when I catch up with Molly! Now I fear that if I drive in behind her I won't be able to learn what she's up to.

At the same time she almost hoped Molly would glance into her rearview mirror as the Cadillac passed by the end of this lane, which, she remembered, curved enough so that the single dwelling there couldn't be seen. If only she would notice Gracie and wave at her in welcome, then Gracie could stop feeling like she was playing a part in a made-for-TV movie!

Now, however, the important thing was to look for a place where she could get off the road and, preferably, be able to hide her own vehicle.

Ah, there, just a short distance away, is what

looks like the end of another lane — perhaps an old logging road? This was more overgrown than the previous one, and she slowed almost to a stop as she studied it. It had obviously not been used for some time, but it appeared to be safe to drive on.

She pulled forward a little more, so she could back in. Just in case she should have to leave in a hurry, she'd already be pointed out, ready to go. *And I'm not about to ask myself why I might have to leave in a hurry.*

She considered the possibility of getting stuck, but she decided that the heavy rain had been long enough ago that it shouldn't be a problem — especially since this didn't appear to be a boggy area.

At least I hope it's not!

Looking out at the vines, bushes and briars, Gracie was thankful she'd put on jeans and a chambray shirt this morning. They were her working clothes and now they'd help keep brambles from ripping her skin.

What she was wearing was actually a pair of Elmo's much-washed jeans. She'd never considered trying them on while he was living, but was surprised to later find they fit so well, and were so comfortably soft.

Was there anything she should take with her? Partly because she so frequently picked up friends as a favor, Gracie made a point of keeping Fannie Mae's interior free of clutter. But she did keep in the trunk those things Elmo had always insisted must be there. Opening it, she saw her flashlight, jumper cables, small fold-up shovel and well-stocked first-aid kit, right where they should be.

There was also a strong, lightweight rope she'd neglected to remove after using it when bringing home her eight-foot Douglas fir from a friend's choose-and-cut tree farm way back last Christmas season. And here was that small, pocket-sized first-aid kit that actually belonged up front in the glove compartment!

She pocketed the latter and picked up the flashlight — not that she anticipated needing its brightness on this lovely day, *but it doesn't hurt to have it, even though I don't expect to use it either for its light or as a weapon!*

She started to pull down the trunk, then decided to reach back in for the rope, which she looped over her left shoulder. Making as little noise as possible — which she assured herself was not identifiable since a truck was passing by on the macadam road at that moment — she shut the trunk, drew in a deep breath and started in the direction of the cabin.

Chapter Six

Gracie was struck by the silence — *well, it's not truly silence, except in the sense of human-generated sounds. The leaves are whispering above me, moved by a breeze I can't even feel. And there's the scurrying rustle of that squirrel over there — though he's now stopped to check on what I'm doing in his territory.*

She also heard the *rat-a-tat-tat* of a woodpecker she couldn't locate as she kept walking. And, of course, there were songbirds warbling in the beauty of the day, along with a crow raucously cawing, perhaps warning of a stranger in their woods.

These sights and sounds registered only peripherally, however, for her thoughts were mostly on what the next few minutes might bring. *I shouldn't be doing this alone, I should have Herb or someone with me. How could I have been so careless as to not pick up my purse before leaving the church?*

I have only vague ideas of what might take place — and I'm hoping — in fact, rather desperately hoping — that Molly is completely in-

nocent of wrongdoing. Or of wrong-planning.

And of course that blanketed something could be anything — anything at all, like. . . .

But she couldn't think of any reasonable object it might be; Molly would not have wrapped a blanket around a rug, for example. She had almost never come here with Frank, so far as Gracie knew — so it seemed improbable that she'd taken to bringing things to spruce up the place.

And there was that phone number at Tish's, and Miltie's seeing one of the twins going into Molly's house this morning. Again, there could be an innocent reason for that, nothing more sinister than stopping for a cup of coffee and a friendly chat.

Why did that not seem likely?

Here I am, God, judging others — and Your word tells us that as we judge others, we also will be judged. Just because I don't often go out of my way to have a "friendly chat" with Molly doesn't mean that Tish should feel the same way.

But You know, God, I'm here mostly because I have the feeling that You got me to Tish's, then to Molly's, because You wanted me there. And, frankly, I'm scared right now, for I haven't the faintest idea what I'm going to do or say.

It's sort of like that anthem for Sunday, isn't

it? In faith I'm coming here, and in hope — oh, how I'm hoping I'm doing what You want me to! And in love, or "charity," as well, for Tish is my friend, and she's Your child every bit as much as I am.

She was mentally singing the next two lines, "We bring our happiness and pains/We bring our losses and our gains. . . ."

Please, Lord, help the gains to outweigh the losses today. She came around another clump of laurel — and the cabin was in view. She was reminded of her reaction at seeing it for the first time, for in truth it was far more than what she'd expected as "a cabin in the woods."

Looking around, she wondered if it might even have once been a farmhouse, for those trees must have been planted, not being nearly large enough to have been part of an original forest.

She tried to make her approach stealthily, moving as carefully as possible from behind one tree to another, and from bush to thicket. The house's foundation was almost two feet high, so she could only hope Molly wouldn't see her as she bent over and ducked her head down while crossing the last twenty or thirty feet to the front porch. *I should be safe unless she's right here by a window, looking out. And I would have stayed close to the building even if she hadn't parked with the front bumper so near.*

Gracie dropped to her hands and knees to keep concealed while going up these steps at the side of the porch. She then got to her feet, back pressed against the wall between the window and the screened door.

From here she could see into the Chrysler parked nearby. Yes, that Indian-type blanket was still on the backseat, but it was now crumpled and obviously empty, just lying there.

Okay, so my guess is that whoever or whatever was wrapped in it is now inside the house. And, if that's Tish, she must have been able to walk, or at least bear some of her own weight, for I doubt that Molly could carry her. She'd probably have had to use that blanket if she'd dragged her inside.

Wouldn't she?

It was then that Gracie heard Molly's voice, at first not totally audible, then becoming more so. ". . . So what if you did see me cutting off Marge's hydrangeas? I didn't destroy her plant, did I?

"What was it to you, anyhow? I didn't take any of yours — though I have no idea why anyone, even you, would want just one big old snowball bush like yours."

The voice receded, then became stronger again. "Why couldn't you have just dropped it, Tish? How *dare* you come to me and say if I don't confess you'll report me? What did it matter what I was going to do with them? Of course I. . . ."

Of course what? Gracie wondered. She listened intently.

". . . Can't take all — not this year. It would be too obvious . . . Didn't plan on Rick's mini-ones at all . . . No competition. . . ."

Ah, no competition because, as far as I know, she has no miniatures like Rick's. I don't recall anyone's even entering those in the fair until last year — so I don't know if there will be others this one, either, now that his are gone.

"I've worked so hard," Molly stated. "You have no idea how much time I spend with my floriculture, how much equipment it takes, and the electricity for all those shelves and trays of hydrangeas in my basement."

So that's why all those flowers and plants are filling the sunroom! The electric power's been off too long, so she had to lug every one of those plants, hundreds of them, it looked like, up those stairs.

". . . Up until now, there's been. . . ."

She must be pacing back and forth in there,

114

since I'm only intermittently hearing her distinctly. Gracie had to shift position a little, being extra careful about making no sound, since she had no way of knowing how near to the door Molly was.

But Tish is obviously in there, for Molly spoke to her by name — so why isn't she responding? Is she unconscious? Gagged? What?

Footsteps were approaching the door, and Gracie held her breath. She was as flat against the wall as possible, and so close — too close, as Molly sighed — maybe only eighteen inches from her.

"How I wish you hadn't come to my house, Tish! It's not that I don't like you, you understand. It's nothing personal, you know, but you should never have seen my hydrangeas.

"Because I know you can't be as dumb as you sometimes seem to be. You *understood* what you were seeing — I could tell from your expression." There were sounds Gracie couldn't recognize. Then Molly spoke again. "So you've made a real mess for yourself, Tish, getting me into this spot where I now have no choice."

No choice about what? I want to help Tish, but what's already happened to her? The most worrisome thing is that she's made no sound —

115

not speaking nor thrashing around or banging or anything.

Gracie shivered, forced suddenly to consider the possibility that her friend was silent because she was already beyond help — in which case Gracie should be getting back to the car, pronto!

It was almost unbearable — both what Gracie was experiencing and what she was imagining — which was certainly lurid enough! Only with difficulty did she control the involuntary gasp that accompanied the thought, *What really happened to Frank Maginnis?*

She closed her eyes for a moment, feeling weak, there on the porch, glued against the wall. She could not leave until she knew for sure what condition Tish was in.

What am I doing here, God? Why didn't You send Herb, or Rick, or someone who might have a better idea what to do now? Frankly, Lord, I'm scared — as though You didn't already know that! And what made me think of poor Frank?

Molly's voice was now more gentle as she moved away from the screen door. Gracie heard her footsteps on the bare floor, and she was almost crooning, as one would to a small child. "It's all right, little Tish, this whole thing isn't going to hurt at all, I promise.

"That's because you always have been so gentle, so cooperative and gracious. You accepted and drank that special sleepy-tea I brewed with no question, and now it's just a matter of time, you know. Just a matter of time until your little nap becomes a lasting slumber."

How long does Tish have, God? Should I just barge in there? But if I rush in, what can I do once I'm there? How can I rescue her with Molly here? Does she have a weapon? Maybe a gun? After all, this was Frank's hunting cabin.

She looked down at the flashlight in her hand, and with the other fingered the rope looped over her shoulder. *I'm willing to help, God, but let's face it, I'm no David — nor a Deborah, either! I don't even have a sling, let alone an army to fight with me, and for You. I'm just an ordinary woman — one who, incidentally, is supposed to right now be preparing a meal for the Willow Bend Rotary Club!*

Poor Eleanor McIver, over there at the church plugging away without me! How worried she must be now! But my duty is here, and that's why You brought me.

Those Rotarians and their spouses would have to survive on whatever was there — and as well-fed as many of them were, they could survive very well if some of the meal's extra trimmings were missing.

Okay, God, I think I may have a game plan — and I hope it's what You want from me — though it sounds sort of screwy, not at all what I'd normally come up with. You know even better than I do that this is something I can't possibly get away with unless You are right here beside me.

Reversing her path down and away from the porch, Gracie was soon back into the woods she'd so recently left. She didn't go far toward her car; instead, she circled around to just beyond the bend in Molly's lane.

She glanced at the flashlight in her hand, realizing this would look decidedly suspicious here in the middle of the day. And, yet, she didn't want to leave it somewhere, for she might need it to — protect herself? To help with — with *what?* To get Tish safely to the emergency room was her major goal, even if she had no idea how much time remained to save her life.

Her pockets were much too shallow for such a large light — but this particular pair of work pants had a loop along the seam on the outside of her right thigh. She remembered Elmo sticking the handle of his hammer through it when he needed both hands free for whatever he was doing.

Yes! It fits! *Okay, God, I guess maybe I*

needed that reassurance, too. As You know, I seldom wear these pants, but here I am — and my light, my weapon-if-I-need-it, fits as though the loop were especially made for it.

She drew in a deep breath and courageously started walking toward the cabin, but as she rounded the curve she became aware of the pounding in her chest. *Is this what a panic attack feels like? If so, I'm sure grateful for not normally being subject to them!*

I know, Lord, You promised to be with me always, even to the ends of the world — and right now I'm calling upon You to be with me as I go up this driveway — as I attempt to talk with Molly. I've got some ideas, but don't know what will happen, or what to say or do.

I'll be trying really hard to keep open to Your leading, to Your guidance.

It had become difficult to swallow, but she forced herself to do so. Even in these sneakers, her steps upon the gravel and dirt seemed overly loud.

Deciding the best approach was not to go up onto the porch unannounced, she called, "Molly — Molly, are you here? It's Gracie." Maybe identifying herself was unnecessary, but it seemed reasonable, almost normal, to say who she was as she started up the four stone-and-cement steps. "I see your car here. . . ."

She heard what sounded like a flurry of activity. Then, as she added, "I need some help," and she saw Molly coming to plant herself on the other side of the screen door, partially blocking her view.

"What are *you* doing here?"

"Well, my car stopped up the road a piece." She wasn't proud of lying about car trouble, but couldn't think of any other way to explain her presence on Molly's porch. "May I come in and use your phone?"

The other woman remained where she was, solidly in front of the doorway, but no longer looking quite as strained. "Sorry, Gracie. Frank used to have a phone here, but I had it taken out."

"Oh." *I guess I shouldn't be surprised, but I'll have to get inside some other way!* Saying nothing more, she reached for the door handle and pulled.

Molly did the same, but not as quickly. The door stood open enough for Gracie to put her foot inside, smile and say, politely, "Could I please have a drink, anyway? I'm so very thirsty."

Molly continued holding on to the handle. "Not today, Gracie. I'm — just about to leave."

A quick glance to the right revealed a somewhat worn couch on which she could see someone's legs, definitely female. "I didn't realize you had company — I didn't notice a second car."

Molly became indignant. "Really, Gracie! You are being extraordinarily nosy."

That was certainly true. "But, Molly," Gracie wheedled, "we've been friends for years. Can't you at least get me a glass of water? I'm sorry to be a bother."

Gracie had expected another negative response, but Molly breathed out quickly, heavily, almost a snort. Something seemed to change behind her eyes, just for a split second, then she returned Gracie's "innocent" gaze with an almost-smile. "Oh, all right, wait here for a moment and I'll get you some special tea I brought."

The door was allowed to open completely, and Gracie stepped inside. Seeing that Tish was lying there on the couch, motionless and with eyes closed, Gracie merely asked, "Is she okay?"

Molly shrugged. "She mentioned not having slept well last night, so she just lay down for a few minutes while I was gathering things to take back to Willow Bend. We'll be leaving shortly."

She turned away while speaking and

moved toward the door through which Gracie could see the kitchen stove. As she started to follow, Molly turned back toward her. "I'll be only a moment, so you can wait here."

That's the second time you've indicated that I shouldn't come with you. But, somehow, I don't think that's what I should be doing.

Gracie tagged along, with no mention of ignoring Molly's instructions. Her neighbor was at the counter, her back to Gracie as she reached up into the cupboard for two frosted glasses, and started filling one from a thermos sitting there. The other glass, however, she filled from a different container.

Gracie had a peculiar spasm-like sensation in her stomach, as she wondered if — but it was almost too awful to contemplate — Molly could be attempting to get rid of her, as well. "Do you have any ice, Molly?"

Gracie moved closer to where her hostess was screwing the wide cap back onto that less than half-full two-liter bottle. As Molly held out one of the glasses toward her, Gracie said, "I'm spoiled by civilization — I like hot drinks hot and cold drinks cold." She said it lightly, although she knew she'd never felt a heavier suspicion.

A rather self-satisfied look crossed Molly's face as she assured Gracie, "Oh, yes, there's ice. It's just not as freshly made as what you're used to."

Is she saying that in case I might notice an off-flavor in my drink? "Well, I'd appreciate a couple cubes, since you have them."

Molly turned back around to the refrigerator, then opened the freezer unit to remove a plastic ice tray.

Quickly but cautiously, Gracie switched the position of the two glasses. The glass meant for her was just a bit fuller than the other, but all she had time for now was to hope Molly wasn't aware of that.

If what she gave me — which I've now given to her — was indeed the "special" concoction she mentioned to Tish, isn't it probable that there's some taste, some flavor that could alert her? It was then she noticed gratefully the bottle of lemon juice Molly was picking up from the counter and saying, "Myself, I like this in my tea, with a bit of sugar. Of course, I don't keep fresh lemons out here."

"I do appreciate your bothering with this when I did just barge in on you."

"No bother at all, Gracie." *Molly could hardly be a better hostess than she seems right now. That by itself has to be grounds for alarm, since she certainly didn't want me to come in or follow her here. Please stick by me, God. Help me not to do anything really stupid — or dangerous!*

Molly appeared completely in control. "Here, Gracie, you add the amount of lemon juice and sugar you'd like."

She accepted the bottle, shook it and, unscrewing the lid, held it tilted first against the rim of the glass now intended for Molly. She slowly started to pour some of the juice into it as she glanced up at Molly. "Just say when."

It was only a second before Molly said that was enough, and Gracie then decanted some into her own glass before recapping the container and handing it back. Molly added her own sugar with an iced-tea spoon, and Gracie declined any sweetener.

Molly rinsed the spoon off and placed it, handle down, into the dish drainer, in which was one — *only* one, Gracie noted — tall glass of the type they were using.

Molly seemed relaxed, unhurried as she suggested they sit here in the kitchen, and Gracie agreed, although terribly aware of the passing of time. How dangerous was it to postpone getting Tish to the hospital?

Molly asked about the car, how it had acted before dying on her. Gracie replied that it had been working fine, conking out without any warning. Yes, she was sure there'd been enough gas, and no, she'd had no recent difficulties with it, none at all.

She also stated, quite honestly, that she definitely needed to be on her way, being now overdue at the church. Molly, however, although having made the point earlier of wanting to leave immediately, had turned quite garrulous, discussing anything and everything.

Gracie played along for one crucial reason: although she was terribly concerned about getting help for Tish, she'd noticed Molly's ring of keys lying over on the counter, beyond the refrigerator. If there was any chance at all, she was going to get over there and pick them up.

She still had no good plan for how to get away from there with Tish, but she watched as Molly drank all of the heavily lemon-and-sugar-flavored tea in her glass. When she herself took only sips, Molly urged her to drink up.

It was only when Molly went into the front room for a moment that Gracie stood up, dumped the contents of her glass down the drain, and managed to pocket those keys. She was reseated with her empty glass before the other's return. "How's Tish doing?"

"She's still sleeping soundly — she must have been really tired."

Gracie got to her feet and stretched, then put both empty glasses into the sink as she suggested, "I suppose it's time for all of us to go back."

"Pretty soon — perhaps let her sleep a bit longer. . . ."

"But you said you were ready to leave when I got here, and I've already kept you far too long."

A shrug. "Oh, well, it won't matter much."

Is she waiting for me to become unconscious — as well as for Tish to die? "But don't you have to get your hydrangeas ready to take to the fairgrounds?"

There was a quickly sucked-in breath, and a briefly worried expression crossed Molly's face before giving way to a more composed look. "I know exactly which ones to take, and what vases I'm using."

This offered an excuse to keep the conversation going for another fifteen minutes, which Gracie kept track of on her watch. She *thought* Molly might be slowing down a bit, but it might have been her own desperate desire that whatever had been in that container would begin to take effect. She finally got to her feet, suggesting, "Let's go

126

wake Tish and get started."

Molly shook her head. "I've decided to let her sleep longer, but was just thinking it might be best for you to walk over to the next house, the Johnsons'. They're probably home, and you can make your call from there."

Gracie was trying to figure out how to refuse that suggestion when Molly added quickly, "It's not far if you go through the woods, instead of around by the road."

Is there a reason you want me to go through the woods? Do you know that the stuff you meant for me acts so quickly that I might keel over while wandering around out there by myself? That I might not be found for a very long time — until after I'm dead?

"I'd rather ride back to town with you, Molly. You can drop me off at the church so I can finish helping Eleanor — and I can call the garage from there, to ask them to come for my keys and tow in the car."

She'd walked into the other room and, glancing back, saw Molly's face tighten a little, as though she was trying to keep from yawning. "My apologies — it's not the company." There was the bare hint of a smile. "Maybe it's seeing how well Tish is sleeping that's affecting me."

"It's — strange, sort of. . . ."

"*What's* strange?" A very quick question.

"She hasn't changed position at all since I first saw her." Gracie walked over to the couch and had started to reach out to touch Tish's forehead when Molly stopped her with a sharp, "Leave her alone!" Then she caught herself and gave a little laugh that sounded artificial. "The poor girl said she was awfully tired, so let her sleep!"

"But if she's — sick or something?"

"She didn't say one single word about not feeling well! She just said she was tired."

Gracie laid her hand on Tish's forehead. "She feels *cold*, Molly."

As she reached for Tish's wrist, to check her pulse, Molly's hand nearly slapped hers. "What's with you, anyway? Haven't you ever seen anyone sound asleep before?"

"I'd like to take her to the hospital, Molly. There's got to be something very — *wrong* with her." *Molly's scornful laugh doesn't sound right, either.* "How about the two of us carrying her to your car?"

"Gracie, Gracie, Gracie. . . ." Molly sounded like a too-long-indulgent mother addressing a not-very-bright child. "If you're in that much of a hurry to get back to town that you can't wait for her to wake up naturally, then go ahead and *leave*. Remember that Tish is *my* guest, not yours, and I want her to . . ." she again gave that controlling-a-yawn grimace, ". . . to get more sleep if she needs it."

Oh, Lord, I don't know if it's safe to tell her yet about switching those glasses. Is most of that liquid still in her stomach? If only I had some idea of how badly Tish needs immediate medical treatment! Am I risking her life by waiting to confront Molly? And have I risked Molly's, too?

Chapter Seven

Hoping that her compulsion to get treatment for Tish as soon as possible was God's answer, she turned fully toward Molly. "Help me get her into your car right away."

Molly's eyes narrowed, and her face became one glowering frown. "You've always been one bossy broad, Gracie Parks, but you have no right to make demands of me!"

Does everyone think I'm that bossy, God? But she couldn't waste another second on inconsequential thoughts like that. "Perhaps I do, Molly. If she dies, you will be up on murder charges. I promise to see to that personally."

"What nonsense!" But there seemed to be a slight twitch at the corner of her mouth, as though she'd nearly not succeeded in controlling a laugh. "You are insane!"

Gracie looked right at her, and knew she'd have to let her adversary know that her secret was one no longer. "How long does it take to work, Molly?"

"I have no idea what you're talking about!"

"Then you have nothing to fear if I tell you that whatever her fate may be, you will follow her."

"What drivel!"

"Maybe not."

There was a slightly sucked-in breath. "What do you mean?"

"For one thing, Molly, I wanted a drink of water, not what you gave me."

This brought a bit of reddening to her cheeks. "You asked for a drink, and I gave you some of my tea. You added your own lemon juice, if you recall."

"So I wouldn't recognize the strange taste."

"I don't know what you are talking about."

Dear God, let me be doing the right thing. "So you have no reason then to be disturbed when I tell you about having switched the glasses in the kitchen while you were getting out the ice cubes."

Molly's eyes became so huge that Gracie saw white clear around the pupils. "You . . . what?"

"But you have nothing to fear, of course, since what you poured into the glass for me was perfectly harmless."

"How *dare* you?"

If this weren't so deadly, it would be laughable! As it was, there was nothing humorous about this mess. "How much time do you have, Molly? How long after Tish drank your potion did she pass out?"

Molly glanced at her watch. "How long . . . ?"

"Tish was already unconscious before I got here."

Molly ran for the backyard, and Gracie followed, hearing the gagging, as she attempted to empty her stomach — which proved ineffective. Molly's face was white and strained as she looked around. "Do you know what you've *done?*"

Gracie nodded slowly. "I have done to you what you planned for me — what you'd already done to Tish." She was tempted to add what she did not actually know, though beginning to suspect, *What you may have done to your husband.*

But she couldn't give Molly a moment of respite, a chance to think of anything but the present. "You've already tried to cover several yawns these last few minutes."

The distraught woman turned toward the doorway and went back inside, holding onto the doorjamb for a moment as though needing its support. She stared with bulging eyes across the tops of the kitchen counters before rushing into the other room, accidentally bumping into the corner of the old-fashioned desk as she went.

"And you're already running into things," Gracie pointed out. "How much longer can you even remain on your feet?"

A sob came from Molly as she stumbled around, stopping at the table in the corner. When Gracie asked what she was doing, she cried, "My keys. I don't know where they are — where did I put them?"

"Tell you what, Molly," Gracie offered, almost conversationally, "if you help me get Tish in the car, I'll help you find the keys."

Molly didn't even glance her way, just kept on with her searching, even getting down on her knees to reach under the couch. Dust and dirt, even mouse droppings came out — but she was obviously not going to find what she was hunting for.

"I don't know where they *are,*" she whimpered in the voice of a frightened child. "Where can they *be?*"

"Look, Molly," Gracie was trying to be firm, to get her to focus, "we have to get Tish into the car — get her to the hospital. It is critical — time's probably running out. . . ."

"What about *me?*" she cried. "You don't care about me!"

"You're wrong about that, Molly. You really are." *How can I get you to understand that?* "Even if we get you back to the hospital in time to save your life, if Tish dies, you'll spend the rest of your life in prison, for her murder.

"I care very much that you will not have to face that — believe me, your life will be nothing like your previous one if that should happen."

Molly looked around wildly. "My keys — I never lose my keys!"

"Don't worry about them right now. We've got to get Tish into the car!"

"What good will that do? Without the keys. . . ." Tears were running down her cheeks as she yanked open drawers in the desk and the end table.

"Help me move Tish." Gracie spoke firmly, making this a command, which she thought for a moment was going to work as Molly took two steps in that direction.

But then she stopped there in the middle of the room, looking around, her gaze hardly focusing. "It's no use. Unless I find the keys. . . ."

Gracie walked over to put her hands on the other's upper arms and shake her. "Settle down, Molly!"

"That's easy for *you* to say. *I'm* the one

134

who's going to die!"

"But you don't need to die, not if you're sensible, not if you help me with Tish."

"But — the keys. . . ."

"I think I know where they are."

This time she'd got Molly's attention. "Tell me."

"Not yet, Molly. Not till you help me put Tish into your car."

A demented look crossed Molly's face as she dug her long nails down Gracie's right cheek. And then both of her hands, her very strong hands, were tightening around Gracie's throat, trying to strangle her.

Gracie tried to pull Molly's fingers away, but couldn't, so she balled her fist and punched into the woman's stomach with every ounce of her strength. Molly doubled over, hands covering the pain-filled area, and Gracie, her face burning, stepped back, standing in what was unconsciously a boxer's stance. She had her fists ready if needed, waiting to see what was about to come next.

She was surprised, amazed even, when Molly began to cry noisily, blubbering, "You hit me — you hurt me. . . ."

She must be further out of it than I realized. "This is your last chance, Molly; either you shape up and help me get Tish into the car or you will die. It is as simple as that."

"I — hurt too much. . . ." She was whimpering.

Gracie couldn't afford to give sympathy. "That's only the beginning of what will happen if you do not voluntarily help me, Molly."

She looked up. "You are a cruel, vicious woman!"

It probably takes one like that to accuse others of behaving similarly. "I'd like to save your life, as well as Tish's. If that means I'm cruel, so be it."

"Where are my keys?"

"Help me carry Tish. . . ."

"No!"

"Then my answer's *no,* also." And she stepped quickly to the side as Molly started for her, then crashed into the table at the foot of the couch, knocking that over and causing a pottery lamp to hit the floor and shatter.

Molly began swearing, a stream of invective so varied and long that Gracie was appalled, especially since she'd never before heard this woman use even a relatively mild cussword. "All right, now that you have that out of your system, let's get Tish to the car."

But she realized from Molly's body language that, at this point, she was even more furious than before.

Gracie kept an eye on Molly as she went back to the couch. As far as she could tell, Tish's breathing and pulse rate were unchanged. *But what do I know about any of this, God? Please give me wisdom. I so desperately need it. I don't see how I can move her by myself, but if there's no other way, I'll do my best.*

Still, she had to try once more with Molly, who was rummaging in drawers that she'd already looked in. "Come help me," she requested in as calm a voice as she could manage. "As soon as we get Tish into the car, we will all leave for the hospital, and I hope we'll save both your lives."

"We can't. I don't know how to start the car without those keys. . . ."

"But I'm sure where they are — I told you that." They were repeating themselves endlessly. But Gracie was not going to produce the keys until she knew Tish would get to the hospital.

Molly tenaciously refused to give assistance, so, abandoning her for the moment, Gracie hurried out to Molly's car and opened both back doors before returning to the living room.

She'd seen firemen on TV carrying lifeless bodies or unconscious people over their shoulders. (She thought that was called a dead-man carry but would shove the phrase out of her mind.)

Deciding it was her only hope of being able to deliver Tish to the car, she sat down beside her and tried to raise the upper part of Tish's body. But the drugged woman's head sagged backward at an alarming angle!

Even if I can somehow carry her out there, God, can I get her inside? And yet, by just sitting here thinking about it I'm losing time — time I don't have enough of.

Oh, PLEASE, Lord, make Molly help me when I ask one more time. "Molly," she kept her voice soft, gentle, "I know how worried you are and I want to help you — but I must also help Tish. We can help both of you if we work together.

"Please, Molly, come help me carry her — and I promise that we'll then find the keys and will immediately leave for the hospital."

Molly stayed where she was, across the room, and Gracie waited, perfectly still, praying. *Make her responsive, Lord. I'm afraid to say more, afraid she may refuse out of spite, if nothing more.*

Slowly, uncertainly, almost clumsily, Molly did start toward them, saying nothing. Gracie suggested, "If you'll take her legs, Molly, I think I can manage her head and shoulders."

Gracie lifted the top of Tish's body, head against her chest and, backing up, started for the door, praying that Molly, holding Tish by the ankles, would follow along.

And she did. It was awkward, and Gracie was surprised at how heavy Tish seemed to be. *Of course this is all dead weight* — but she immediately revised that mental mention of *dead* again!

They crossed the living room and went through the doorway and over the wooden porch floor with its peeling paint. "We'll have to lift her a bit higher as we go down the steps," Gracie said — and was grateful that Molly seemed to be making some effort to do so.

Thank goodness she owns a big car, too, with wide doors, she thought. Yet she still was hardly able, carrying her friend, to back up, doubled over, in order to enter it. Laying Tish's shoulders and side finally on the seat, Gracie exited through the far door, pulled Tish farther in, and closed the heavy door. She then went around the car to assist Molly, secure the seat belts, and close that door as well.

"And, now, I demand my keys." Molly was both belligerent and wobbly. The will power that was keeping her going was admirable, Gracie had to acknowledge, wondering when she would collapse.

Gracie had expected that, so she patted Molly's shoulder. "I'll get them." Since she didn't think she should let the other woman know they'd been in her pocket all this time, she hurried back inside the house and locked the back door.

Molly was just coming in as she returned to the living room, so Gracie said, "I'll meet you at the car."

Molly tried to stop her, again demanding what belonged to her. But Gracie walked past her and got in the driver's seat. She waited until then to remove the keys from her pocket, insert the correct one into the ignition, and start the motor.

She'd expected Molly to be right behind her when she got to the car, but now she saw her pause in the doorway before running out onto the porch.

"Get out of my car!" Gracie could not mistake what was in Molly's hands.

She expects no argument about that, since she's carrying a rifle, undoubtedly one of those Frank used for hunting. She was coming down the steps on the left side of the porch, those which Gracie had crept up so cautiously what now seemed like eons ago.

It could have actually been even less than

an hour. Gracie couldn't take her eyes off what was going on in front of her even long enough to glance at her watch. Molly came to a stop directly in front of the car, raising her weapon. "Get out of my car or I'll shoot you!"

She very well may do that whether I stay in or get out of the car. She could so easily dump Tish somewhere before she gets to the emergency room, then make up some explanation as to how she'd been poisoned! Gracie swallowed hard — and put the car in gear. *Don't let me hurt her, Lord, at least not too badly,* she prayed silently — and proceeded to do the only thing she could think of that might save both Tish and herself.

Gracie moved the car faster than she'd intended — and Molly, squinting through the rifle's telescopic lens, didn't realize her danger until its bumper pinned her against the house.

She screamed, perhaps with pain — certainly with surprise and horror. Gracie stopped the forward movement, but made no effort to back up, to release her. Molly, trying to steady the gun, yet needing to hold onto the front of the car because of the pressure on her legs, shouted, "I *will* kill you."

Realizing this was all-too-possible, Gracie called back, "The only thing saving you from being crushed to death this instant is my foot on the brake. If you shoot me, the pressure will come off of this pedal — and your death will be much more horrible than mine.

"You will be slo-o-owly crushed, squeezed until your insides and outsides become a shapeless, gruesome, ugly mass!" *I have to make this so revoltingly vivid she won't be able to bring herself to shoot me.*

There was silence for a moment before, in a small voice, Molly said, "Gracie?"

"What?"

She lowered the gun, partially laying it on the car's hood. "Back up," she pleaded, tears coming down her cheeks. "*Please* back up. . . ."

"I *can't*, Molly — I can't trust you. If I let you go, you'll kill me — and Tish. You know you will."

"No! No, I won't."

She sounded sincere — perhaps really meant it — at this moment. "Then throw away that gun. Throw it off there toward the woods — just as far as you can."

That was apparently more than Molly could bring herself to do. She just stood there, shaking her head. Gracie eased the pressure on the brake, and Molly screamed again as the heavy vehicle moved forward an infinitesimal amount. "Gracie! *Stop . . . !*"

I'm the one, God, who can't stand even to step on a worm, and feel terrible when a bird flies in front of my car and is killed when it collides with the windshield. But now — now I'm in the position of having to do this to a woman I used to consider a friend. "Throw away that rifle!"

For a moment it seemed as though Molly would obey, but then she looked back at Gracie. "Back up!" she demanded. "You're hurting me."

"That's because you haven't thrown away the gun. Do it immediately, or your own vehicle will destroy you!"

This was no time to feel sorry for her, but Gracie almost did. "I'm going to count to five, then let the car crush you if that's what you want."

"Don't do that!" She was almost hysterical, but still holding on to that rifle, still undoubtedly planning to use it. "Back up — back up now!"

"One!" *Is the gun loaded? Frank always prided himself not only on his deer kills, but on his precautions when it came to gun safety. He'd certainly have removed any shells and thoroughly cleaned this gun. Molly never hunted with him. Had she ever even tried to put a shell in the chamber? Does she have any idea about releasing the safety-mechanism?*

"Two!" Molly had remained in the house longer than Gracie had expected, then come out holding that gun in her hands. She was handling it clumsily now, though at this range she could hardly miss her target.

"Three!" Gracie felt perspiration forming on her forehead. *Perspiration? That's sweat! I don't want to have to crush her, Lord, and I don't believe I would if it was just me here in the car. But for Tish?*

Please don't let me have to make this decision!

She had to clear her throat before saying the next word. *It's got to be loud and forceful — strong enough so there's no doubt in her mind that I will follow through.*

"FOUR!" And this time she added, equally loudly, "This is your last chance, Molly. When I say the next number, whether or not you shoot me, whether or not you then throw away the gun, you will die."

Tears were streaming down Molly's cheeks and she was sobbing. "Let me — go!"

"I will not permit you to kill Tish!" *Dear Lord, make her throw that away!*

The weapon wavered a little more, and Molly hugged it close to her chest for a moment — then tossed it to her right. *It's not very far, God, but it's enough. Thank You.*

Gracie took the car out of gear, but didn't move it — just reached for the rope there on the seat beside her. She wished this were her own Cadillac, since she had continued doing as Elmo always insisted, keeping a sheathed knife in the glove compartment.

"In case of an accident, in case something happens that you can't release your seat belt, get out this hunting knife and free yourself," is what he'd said. Did Frank also believe in doing this? They'd thought so much alike concerning so many things — used to be as close as brothers — and this *had* been Frank's car.

She reached across and opened the glove compartment, her hand searching for — *Yes! Here it is!*

Molly was calling to her, reminding her that she'd fulfilled her part of the bargain by throwing away the weapon, and she expected the car to be moved. "Release me right now! Then come *out* here."

"I'll be right there." She was cutting off a number of three- to four-foot lengths of the rope, using one of these to tie vertically against her still-bleeding cheek a thick pad of folded tissues she'd taken from the box on the seat.

"What — are you doing?" For just a moment Molly had appeared almost amused by Gracie's bizarre appearance. Now, wide-eyed with apprehension, she watched as Gracie laid two of the other pieces of rope on the hood and approached with the third.

"Give me your hands." She reached for Molly's right one, which her neighbor immediately pulled back and held behind herself. Gracie grabbed the left one and held on tight, even though Molly strained to pull away.

Thank goodness I remember those days so long ago when I helped our son get his merit badges in Boy Scouts! These knots have to hold securely!

It worked well indeed, she thought with satisfaction a little later. In struggling to release her left one, Molly had brought her right hand forward. Gracie captured that one as well, succeeding in binding them tightly together, behind her.

Her captive's vocal tirade continued, but Gracie ignored it as much as possible. She did promise Molly, however, that she would soon be released from the viselike pressure of the car securing her against the house. Gracie supported her as they moved slowly around the front of the car and the open door finally to sit on the front seat.

Gracie realized in time when Molly made an attempt to kick her as she was being maneuvered into the car. "If you try anything like that even one more time, Molly, I swear I will pull you out and leave you along the highway while I take Tish to the hospital!"

"You wouldn't."

"Try me and see!" Her voice and manner were grim. "I will *not* let Tish die if there's anything I can do to prevent it."

Taking the keys from her pocket, Gracie walked around the back of the car and, getting in and closing the door, started the engine and backed around in the small, graveled area.

They were soon off the poorly maintained road and back on the paved highway. "I'm taking you two directly to Keefer Memorial Hospital," Gracie said, still aware of her own aching face — and also of a surprising sense of exhaustion.

But it was only another minute or two until she pulled to the side, turned off the engine, removed the keys, and got out of the car. Molly looked and sounded scared as she demanded, "What are you doing? Why are you stopping here? We have to get there right away!"

Chapter Eight

She didn't trouble to answer as she slammed the door and ran out into the road, flailing her arms. She'd seen the huge white tractor-trailer at a distance, which was being rapidly eaten up, and now she prayed, *Dear Lord, please make the driver decide to stop!*

Please let him be willing to call Keefer Memorial for us, alerting them to the poison emergencies I've got here. If they're on the alert and ready for us, that could give them a little extra time to make sure Tish pulls through.

The driver didn't at first seem to be slowing, so she ran toward him down the middle of the road, waving. She was shouting, also, until she recognized the fact there was no use wasting her breath since he probably couldn't hear her.

But then she heard the power brakes, and saw the right turn signal start to flash. *He's stopping! Oh, thank You, God — he is stopping!*

The trucker started rolling down his

window even before he pulled completely off of the road. He looked not only concerned, but shocked. "What *happened?*" His quick glance toward the parked car seemed to puzzle him. "You were in a — an accident?"

She shook her head. "No, not an accident, but I was wondering — could you please call 911?"

"Sure." Yet that seemed to confuse him more. "But it's — not an accident?"

She'd forgotten how awful she must look — all that blood on her neck and shoulder and blouse, and that makeshift bandage bound to her face with a rope! "I have two passengers who've been poisoned. One's in extremely serious condition — though still hanging in there the last I checked.

"I must alert someone that I'll have them at Keefer Memorial's emergency room within ten minutes."

He was punching numbers into his phone as she talked, then handed it out the window to her before opening the door and stepping down to the road.

"This is Grace Parks," she began. "I'm from Willow Bend, and I want to report that I'm on my way to Keefer Memorial Hospital's emergency room with two patients who have been poisoned — one, at least, being in very serious condition, and unconscious for a long time.

"No, I'm not certain what the poison was. It was brewed into a tea — so I believe it could have been from a plant. But it also could have been some sort of sedative.

"Please ask them to have a gurney waiting for us — and, also, could you contact the police chief at Willow Bend — Herb Bower, that is. Tell him that the most seriously ill patient is Tish Ball."

The man beside her, Jake (according to the name on his shirt), was watching the scene with disbelief.

Meanwhile, the 911 dispatcher was asking for verification information. Gracie gave her current location along with the route she'd be taking to the hospital. Then she brought the call to an end.

"Please, though, ask that the police come to the ER, or, at least, that their hospital security people meet us," she added.

Gracie had been so preoccupied that she'd hardly noticed the mud-brown Ford pickup slowing, then stopping opposite her. Lester Twomley, another member of her church choir, was running across the road. "Gracie! Are you all right?"

"I think so — but Tish and Molly aren't. They've been poisoned, and I'm taking them to the hospital."

He was a short man, no taller than she was, and he was looking into her eyes compassionately as he raised his left hand, indicating her battered face.

"Molly scratched me," she responded to his unspoken question.

"*What?*" His open face showed shock, horror, and puzzlement all at the same time. "Why?"

She sighed. "It's too long a story for now, Les. All I can say is that I was tying her up after I made her throw away the hunting rifle she was about to kill me with."

Jake stared at her. "And you're trying to save her life?"

"Especially Tish's!" The urgency of that mission almost overwhelmed her as she headed back toward Molly's car. "I've got to get her to the hospital."

Lester was right beside her, ignoring Molly and craning his neck to see into the backseat. "I'm going with you."

"I appreciate the offer, Les, but there's no room. Tish is out cold in the back, as you can see."

"There's room!" he contradicted. "I'll hold her in my arms if I have to, but I *am* going with you." Then he glanced at his pickup, said, "I'll be back in a second," and ran to get some things from the front seat and to lock his car doors.

Jake was in his cab, apparently waiting to make sure he wasn't needed any more. Les held up his own cell phone as he ran back. "Thanks for the help! I'll try to take it from here."

Gracie had already returned Jake's phone and now he nodded, easing his rig forward, and shouted, "I'll be prayin' for you, Gracie Parks!"

Already in the car and with the motor running, she called back her thanks, then turned to see Les, who'd put his briefcase on the floor, lifting Tish's head and shoulders from the seat so he could slide in and close the door. "She's — totally limp."

Gracie was pulling onto the highway and gaining speed. "I know. She's been like that ever since . . ." she glanced toward Molly, across from her, slumped against the door. She reached to grab her shoulder. "Molly, can you hear me?"

Her head moved slightly, but she might already be unconscious. Her body slid a bit as the car straightened on the highway, and Gracie pushed her back, so the shoulder belt would help keep her upright. Her gaze met that of Les's in the rearview mirror. "Is there any chance you could hold on to her collar or something? I'm afraid she'll bang her head on the window or fall over on me. Then I'd like you to make a call for me."

"Sure." He slid out of his own shoulder harness, leaving just the seat belt to secure him and Tish as he leaned forward to do as she'd requested. "Now what?"

She gave him Herb Bower's number. "Hi, Lucille, this is Les Twomley. Could Gracie Parks and I speak with Herb?" He spoke slowly and in a somber tone.

Gracie could hear only one end of the conversation. "Herb, it's Les. I'm on the way to Keefer Memorial with Gracie, who's driving Molly's car.

"Both Molly and Tish are unconscious — they've been poisoned, according to Gracie . . . I don't know the details, but yeah, Gracie *seems* okay — except for her face. Well, it seems that Molly scratched her — pretty bad I'd guess, from what I can see. I hope they check her, too, at the hospital."

Gracie reached up to adjust the rearview mirror. *No wonder both Jake and Les looked at me that way, assuming I'd been in an accident!* Her involuntary gasp alarmed Les, so she reassured him, "I just saw my reflection!"

He gave her a quick grin while telling Herb, "Yep, I think Gracie's doing all right. She just saw herself in the mirror and was

153

totally shocked at how awful she looks!"

Then he was back to business. "We've called 911 and they're alerting the hospital, but she wanted to let you know what was happening."

"Ask him to tell Tish's husband. And Tyne, too," Gracie requested. "And, also, if he has time, could he call Eleanor at the church? That poor soul's probably going crazy with worry about me by now, as well as Tish. And she's had to shoulder the entire burden of preparing for that Rotary dinner tonight.

"I said I'd be away for a few minutes when I left there, so she may have called Uncle Miltie and others. If she has, someone better call them, too."

Les started to relay that message, but Gracie interrupted him. "On second thought, we should have enough time while driving to call the church, so Herb doesn't have to take care of any of that — though I'd sure appreciate his coming to the hospital if he has time."

She went on. "If he's going by the church on the way there, I'd also like him to stop and pick up my purse. I was so upset about where Tish might be that I didn't even think about needing my wallet or anything."

Les passed that on, then chuckled at the

response. "He says, Gracie, that you have lots of guts, telling an officer of the law that you're out here driving someone else's car without even having your license with you."

She replied dryly, "Right now that statement is much funnier to you guys than to me."

They were nearing town by the time they had Eleanor on the line. She was relieved to hear that Gracie was apparently all right, but horrified by the very brief summary of what had happened to Tish and Molly.

She asked if she shouldn't put them on the prayer chain, and Gracie suggested that she say that both women were very sick and were being taken to the emergency room. "Ask for prayers for healing — for *complete* healing." *Yes, Lord, they do need complete healing, not only in the physical sense but, for Molly, anyway, a healing of her spirit — of her soul and of her emotions.*

Eleanor reassured that the dinner preparations were well underway and that Gracie was doing the right thing in taking their friends to the hospital. She was not to worry about things at the church — at least not until it was time to serve. Then she would be needed!

Gracie asked for the phone after Les put through the call to Marge at the store. "Are

155

you awfully busy right now?"

"Not awfully, awfully, awfully busy, Gracie — just one or two of those 'awfully's,' I'd say. Are you having a problem?"

Gracie never liked to ask for help, but now knew she had to. "I'm afraid so. Both Tish and Molly are sick, and I'm taking them to the ER. That means poor Eleanor's alone there at the church, getting ready for sixty-five Rotarians and guests. Since I'm almost at the hospital, I may not have a chance to make more calls right away, and wondered if you'd try to round up a couple of people to help out, especially with the serving."

"You won't even be back to help with that?"

"I don't know yet how long I'll have to stay here." *Or if I'll be taken to the magistrate's office — or even to jail. After all, I am guilty of poisoning Molly, despite its seeming the only thing to do right then. And if she should die. . . .*

She tried not to think of such a possibility.

Nor of the consequences should that happen.

But these worries didn't go away, so she handed the phone back to Les once again with, "I'd like to talk to my niece in Chicago." He punched in the numbers for her

156

and, getting the District Attorney's office, asked for Carter.

Gracie had the phone again by the time she answered with, "What a nice surprise to hear from you, Aunt Gracie!"

"I'm not sure it *is* nice, dear, under these circumstances. You see, I may be in a bit of a mess."

"Uh-oh. I don't like the sound of this!"

But Carter's voice had that pleasant lilt to it which invited Gracie to share what was going on. "I'm almost to the hospital's emergency room with Tish Ball, who was poisoned by Molly Maginnis — and with Molly, who was poisoned by me."

"Now just a minute! Exactly what does that mean, that you poisoned Molly?"

"Well, I knew for a fact that she'd poisoned Tish so, when she gave me a glass of her brew, I deliberately switched the glasses. So she drank it, instead, and now she's unconscious — and Tish already was and still is. And, though we're hoping and praying, I can't be sure that either or both of them will make it.

"So I figured I needed professional advice before talking to the authorities. I should be doing that, in fact, almost immediately, since I'm pulling into the ER parking lot right now."

She heard a startled exhalation, and then, "Oh, wow! What you need is a good local lawyer for this one!"

"I don't want a 'local lawyer,' dear, just your input. I do have to tell them the truth, don't I? And I do think that I had no alternative at the time, when I switched the drinks, that is."

"How did you know it was poisoned?"

"Well, I hope they'll believe me when I explain that I was eavesdropping and. . . ."

She heard Les's voice from the backseat, "Oh, Gracie, maybe you shouldn't word it that way — even if it's the truth!"

"That's exactly what happened! I was trying to find a way to save Tish, and. . . ."

Carter inserted quickly, "If you won't get a lawyer to be with you, then my best advice is always to tell the truth — but add nothing to the facts. Don't embellish them with anything that could be considered your interpretation. Les is right to say that *eavesdropping* has a negative connotation, so use *overheard* instead."

Gracie had been at the hospital often enough to know she should pull into the curved drive under the projecting roof, but this was the first time she'd been greeted by such a number of people! One of the security guards came around to her opened window. "Ms. Parks?"

"Yes." She nodded. "I'm Grace Parks, the one who asked that you be called. The patients are," and she turned to indicate the backseat first, "Tish Ball, and Molly — Mary, actually — Maginnis. Molly's been unconscious for only a short time — but Tish has been out for a lot longer."

As the nurses and paramedics began to move Tish onto the nearest gurney, Les was identifying her for the staff. Then as Gracie did the same for Molly, with Les suggesting, "How about your going in with them? I'll park the car and join you in a minute."

This is not going to be fun! What she said was, "Thanks, Les. I don't know how I'd have managed without you!"

Her face, even underneath its lopsided decoration, revealed for a second the familiar Gracie grin as he squeezed her hand more tightly than would have been necessary just to help her stay steady on her feet.

It was about to be question-and-answer time, first with the ER staff, then the state police, who got there right after she did.

Yes, she was pretty sure that Tish's dose had been administered while she was yet in Molly's house in Willow Bend — though she had no proof other than that she had looked unconscious when Gracie first saw her, not long after Molly arrived at the isolated house. Yes, she'd seen the Indian blanket, which was still in the car if they wanted to see it, wrapped around Tish before they'd left Willow Bend.

Well, no, she hadn't actually seen Tish in it. Of course not. But someone — okay, something had been wrapped up in it. It had been crumpled and empty on the backseat when she again saw it at the cabin, only a very short time later.

She glanced toward Les as she was told that she'd soon be taken into one of the curtained examination cubicles herself, so they could clean up her face and see just how badly she'd been hurt. He was only a short distance from her, and his solemn gaze made her even more aware of her story and what it must have sounded like to these people.

Herb arrived and walked over to where two state officers had been questioning her. They obviously knew and respected him for they agreed when he asked, "Would it be all right if I listen in? Gracie called me on her way to the hospital and asked that I come."

People were bustling back and forth. And several times Gracie asked for information about Tish and Molly's condition. Tish finally was moved to critical care and, later,

Molly was moved away from ER, but Gracie could learn nothing about exactly where in the hospital they were taking her.

Gracie's own injuries weren't as bad as she'd feared once the dried, clotted blood was gently washed away. There were four fairly deep, several-inch-long scrapes from Molly's fingernails from the forehead down along the left side, and three of those on the right. Though they hurt a lot while being cleaned and dressed, the doctor thought she'd probably not have any lasting disfigurement. He ordered an antibiotic prescription and a tetanus-booster.

It was late afternoon by the time Gracie was allowed to leave, even though she'd kept insisting she was needed back at the church to help with the meal she was supposed to be catering. She'd feared she would be refused permission to leave, but Herb suggested that he would take responsibility for helping both Gracie and Lester pick up their vehicles, making sure, first, that she would be able to drive on her own.

As they walked out together, she asked, "What about Molly's car?"

Les said, "I parked it clear at the end of the lot, so I'd think it could stay as long as she's a patient. But," fishing the keys from his pocket, "I sure don't want these in my possession."

"Me, neither!" Gracie agreed.

Herb reached for them. "My office safe is probably as good a place as any, unless — do you know if she has relatives, Gracie?"

"I suppose she must have, but I never hear her speak of them. And I don't know of special friends."

"Well, I'll call the hospital and have them tell her, as well as make a note on her records where these are."

That was the last the three of them spoke about the day's fiasco, and Gracie was sure the men were trying to spare her. *But once I get to the church, there'll undoubtedly be lots of discussion! Who wouldn't be curious?*

They dropped Les off at his car before Herb took her to get hers. When they arrived at the rutted lane in which she'd partially hidden it, he turned around and parked along the highway, then walked in with her. "Weren't you afraid you might get stuck in here?"

"I was more afraid that Molly would see me — and, most of all, that I might not be able to help Tish."

"You did recognize that you were playing a dangerous game, didn't you?"

"Of course." She took a half-dozen steps

before adding, "But I had this feeling that I had to save her, no matter what. I know that doesn't make sense, but I had no choice."

"I get those feelings, too. For that matter, every good officer I know has them."

She stopped just before opening the car's door. "I suppose in one way it could be looked on as a curse, to live in danger as you do. But I thank God for your willingness to do it."

"Me, too." But then he was looking around this wooded area. "So you walked through the woods there, in that direction?"

"Um-hm. But it's really not much farther to go by the roads. And oh, I almost forgot! I've got to go back there."

"Whatever for?"

"That hunting rifle! I did check it, and removed the shells." She was digging in her pocket and pulled them out to hand to him. "But I left the gun just lying there."

"Drive your car out of here, Gracie, and then we'll walk in to her place to get the weapon."

She nodded. "And we can lock up the place. The way things were going at that time, neither of us thought to do it."

They were entering the house when Gracie asked the question which had been bugging her. "What do you think the chances are that Frank didn't just walk away several years ago?"

"Knowing what we do now, I have serious questions."

"Well, this business today was almost too easy for Molly. How or why would she even have on hand something like that poison unless she planned to use it, or already had used some of it?"

That reminded her of something else, so she led the way to the refrigerator and started to reach in.

"Don't touch that!"

Chapter Nine

Herb's hand was on her arm, pulling it back. "If the refrigerator jar's holding that toxic brew of hers, we can't have your fingerprints on it at all — and not only because they might cover up Molly's!"

She looked at him, startled, then apologized, "That was stupid of me. Thanks."

He nodded grimly, and reached for his cell phone. It was only moments before he was telling the person who answered to send someone immediately to check for fingerprints at the Maginnis house in the woods. Yes, he'd wait right here for them.

"It's good Fanny Mae's out here, Herb, for I really must go." She started back through the living room and then she thought of something else. "I've been wondering how Molly was able to get Tish in here, even though she parked next to the side steps, close to the house.

"I guess Tish may still have been able to stand, perhaps even to walk some, even if she was semi-comatose. I wasn't far behind, but it did take a while to sneak through the woods and to get up on the porch and hear what Molly was saying. I assumed she was just sort of talking to herself while I was eavesdropping — that's *overhearing*, right? But she may have thought Tish was still able to hear her, and she was gloating.

"But, by the time I again walked around through the woods and came down this drive, called to Molly, then got inside, Tish was all the way under — or at least she wasn't making any sound or movement." The scenario was becoming more and more plausible as she shared her theories.

"Unconsciousness didn't take place all at once with Molly, either."

"It could very well have happened that way," he agreed. "Perhaps we'll soon know for sure — if they can pick up prints from the posts holding up the porch roof, or along the side of the house or doorposts, even in or on Molly's car."

Gracie had not had time alone since she arrived at Molly's. Now she welcomed the brief solitude. *Thanks, Lord, for being with me through this almost unbelievable day, and making it possible for Tish — and Molly, too — to get to the hospital.*

Please help the doctors and nurses as they

work with them, and be with Tish, especially, since she was evidently trying to do what she thought was best — going to see Molly privately, giving her the chance to confess and to try to set things right.

And please, God, although this isn't nearly as important, help us to get the dinner ready to serve on time — and everything to go smoothly. I did try to take care of things there — I had the shopping done, and the bread cubed. . . .

Paul Meyer was in the parking lot when she pulled in, and Gracie was almost sure the young minister had been out there pacing, awaiting her arrival. He started to run toward where she parked, close to the building's entrance. "Oh, *Gracie!*" he cried, looking appalled.

She supposed she shouldn't be surprised at that, since she had not mentioned her injuries. "It's not as bad as it looks."

He yanked the door open and reached for her hand. "We've been so worried."

"I know," she said, already on her feet, "but now we're going in there and see what's needed."

He followed her inside, where she was greeted by Marge, hurrying toward her from where she'd been placing a vase of flowers on the head table. "Am I relieved to see you, Gracie! We've all been frantic."

Eleanor, Louise, Marge and April came rushing from the kitchen and they were all speaking at once, asking — demanding answers. She could see how shocked they were at her appearance, but Gracie raised a hand to stop, or, at least, forestall the rush of questions. "My question takes precedence under these circumstances: how's the meal coming along?"

Eleanor beamed. "It's fine, Gracie, it really is. Since the others got here, we're right on schedule."

"How can I thank you?" Gracie choked up. "I was so worried at leaving you in the lurch!"

"You were worried about us? That's nothing compared with our worry about you and Tish!" Marge insisted.

Gracie put an arm around her friend, temporarily ignoring Louise's questions about her face. "We think Tish is going to be okay, but Herb's going back to the hospital before coming here. If anyone can get a straight answer about her condition, he can."

Rocky called a few minutes later, asking for Gracie, yet seemed surprised when, handed the phone by Paul, she was there to answer. "I just received very disturbing information concerning you, Gracie. Are you all right?"

"Now I am, but I wasn't so sure a while ago."

"What happened?"

She hesitated a moment. "Is this Editor Gravino or my friend, Rocky, asking?"

"Your *very* good friend is terribly concerned about and for you, Gracie — but yes, I am an editor, too." There was a pause. "I can no more completely separate those facets of my being than you can your wonderful presence and personality from your ability to sing and cook and — do so well in so many other things."

She nodded, though he couldn't see that. "You're right, Rocky, and I apologize. It's just that, until I get clearance from the police to do so, you realize I can't say anything for publication."

"Understood and honored!"

She knew him well enough to take that as a promise, so filled him in with the bare outline of the unexpected turns — the unexpected turmoil — of her day. "I'm expecting Herb to come before long, Rocky. When you see him, you should be able to ask for the — uh — official or reportable account."

"And then, with his permission, of course, I will hope to get your personal account. With pictures, please."

"I'm — not sure I want pictures. Wait till

you see how I look!"

"Gracie?" His voice was filled with concern again. "Something's wrong?"

She was almost sorry she'd said that, but he'd be aware of it soon enough. "Well, I'd certainly win no beauty contest — as if I ever would, anyway."

"What happened to you?"

"Oh, dear, I've got to get home and change clothes, that I know for certain."

"Gracie!" The volume of his voice had markedly increased. "What happened?" he bellowed.

"Well, Molly was pretty upset with me — to put it mildly. And she clawed my face, that's what happened."

"Stay there!" It was a command that would take no argument from her. "I'm on my way!" And the line went dead.

It couldn't have been more than five minutes before Rocky came barging in the door with Ben Tomlinson, his top photographer, right behind him. "Good heavens, girl," he thundered, "you look awful!"

That struck her so funny that she started to laugh — using facial muscles she hadn't realized were so sore. Wincing just a bit, she lightly replied, "I've heard the old saying about 'something only hurting when I laugh,' but now I realize that can be all too true."

Everyone insisted that Gracie go home immediately, get cleaned up and changed, then return as soon as possible — only if she felt up to it. She herself was of the opinion she should stay and do at least a few tasks to help there, but Rocky, apparently somewhat reassured that she wasn't critically injured, insisted he'd do whatever they told him to if she would just get on her way.

She looked back at the doorway and couldn't help being amused — and honored — seeing the owner-editor of their prestigious eighty-year-old *Mason County Gazette* taking orders from the determined kitchen brigade.

Her uncle had apparently experienced many emotions, but his fear and apprehension turned quickly to delight now at seeing her back home. She felt she could now give him only a very sketchy version of what had transpired, but explained that as soon as she had Herb's permission, she would give him the whole story.

Uncle Miltie's feelings were obviously hurt. "Either you trust me or you don't — and I don't know what I've ever done to make you *not* trust me as to keeping confidences."

"It's not that at all, and you know it! This whole mess is undoubtedly going to end up in the courts, and I have to follow the rules."

"You think I'm gonna go around blabbing to everyone in town whatever you tell me?"

"No, dear, I do not think that. What I do expect is that soon I'll be able to tell you everything — the parts I myself know, that is." She glanced at the clock and winced. "I have to get washed up and changed and back to the church very quickly. As you remember, I'm supposed to be catering that Rotary dinner tonight."

"Okay," he muttered, his displeasure made obvious by his walker preceding him more rapidly than usual, the rear feet thumping down extra hard with each step he took until he flopped down in his favorite recliner.

She settled on just washing up thoroughly instead of taking a shower. She'd planned to wear a skirt and blouse but now, discovering scratches on her legs and arms of which she'd hardly been aware while going through the woods, she put on lightweight pants and a long-sleeved cotton blouse.

It was only as she was brushing her teeth that she remembered having eaten nothing since breakfast. Her stomach rumbled in response to that wayward thought, but she didn't feel hungry even now.

Well, Gracie, she said to her reflection as she brushed her hair and applied lipstick, *you are certainly a memorable sight tonight! Brick-colored streaks down both cheeks, scratches all over, and your hair a major mess.*

But so what? You have a job to do, and you're going over there to do it!

She wheeled around, turned off the bathroom light, marched out through the living room and kitchen and announced, "I'll be home as soon as possible."

She was relieved that his parting send-off was much as usual. "Have a good time, Gracie."

"I'm sure I will, Miltie dear. I always do." That, too, was a familiar response. "Enjoy your programs."

The church parking lot was crowded by the time she got back to the church — and she was instantly reminded of the speed of small-town gossip. Even before she entered the building there were people demanding to know the real story.

She asked Paul, who was just inside the door welcoming people, whether Herb had arrived. He told her there had been a phone call from him; he'd probably be a little late but planned to eat when he got here.

And, no, her pastor had learned nothing

173

regarding either Tish's condition or Molly's!

Thank goodness I'm so busy, she thought while filling a serving bowl of mashed potatoes for each table, *or waiting for Herb to arrive with news would seem like forever.*

Usually she'd be out front doing the actual serving, but she stayed in the background tonight, not wishing to be overwhelmed by the onslaught of local curiosity.

Les stopped in the kitchen when he arrived, just after Paul had given the blessing for the meal. He asked if there was more news but, finding there wasn't, went to sit with friends. Apparently he entered into their conversation without alluding to his part in Gracie's dangerous adventure. At least so far the people at his table weren't gawking in her direction.

You're quite a guy, Lester Twomley, you really are! And I'm glad to have you for a friend!

It didn't seem right for her to stay in the kitchen like this. Gracie usually loved being out there talking to people while she refilled glasses, served coffee and tea, and helped bring bowls and platters back out to the kitchen for seconds.

Instead, she was cutting pies and setting a delicious-looking variety on each tray. Marge, Eleanor and April reported fielding incessant questions concerning Gracie's experiences — but dessert was being served before Herb got there.

He, too, was bombarded with eager demands for all the details as he came around the tables to the kitchen. "I'm going to have to make a very brief announcement, Gracie — although I'd rather not just yet, since there's still so much we don't know."

"Are Tish and Molly going to make it?" She had to get the answer to that one. But was not totally reassured by his answer.

"We think so."

"You're not sure, even now?"

"Tish has moved her arms and legs some, and must be hearing at least a little of what's being said — so we're hoping she continues to improve."

That was not as much as Gracie had hoped for. "Is John with her?"

"Um-hm, and Tyne is, too." Gracie drew in a big breath before asking, "What about Molly?"

Herb's expression tightened. "She hadn't been out as long, as you know, so she's no longer under the influence — at least not too much. She's given a statement denying her part in everything that happened — and is claiming that you brought that poison, Gracie."

"Me?" She hadn't expected that, could never have conceived of it as a possibility! "Why in the world would I do such a thing?"

"She insists you went crazy, coming to her place there in the woods acting absolutely insane, managing to first poison Tish, then her. And *then,* since it didn't work as fast as you'd hoped, you tried to kill her by driving into her with her own car, crushing her there against the house."

"That's absurd!" *Wouldn't everyone agree this couldn't have taken place? Well, that pinning her against the building did take place, but. . . .* "People don't believe that, do they?"

"She's sure hoping they will! Her mind's working overtime with this, and she's showing the staff her poor damaged legs, which she can't walk on since she was attacked by Gracie!"

"Are they badly bruised?"

"Well, yes. . . ."

Her hand moved up to touch the scrapes on her face. "And these?"

"Oh, she readily admits to that. According to her, she had to — she was trying to shake you out of your dementia — trying to make you stop doing what you were doing."

"Good grief!"

"Indeed!" Now he grinned at her. "But I wouldn't lose sleep over that aspect of the case if I were you," he added, heading back toward the doors, where there were a few empty seats.

"Herb?" she called after him. "Thanks for not letting me touch that container."

He turned enough to raise one hand in a semi-salute. "Any time, my good friend."

She wondered if he'd deliberately and smilingly said that so loudly that everyone would hear him refer to her as his friend — and remember it once Molly's version got out.

She was fairly sure of her hunch when he stated, just before sitting down next to Rocky, "I have an announcement to make, if you don't mind. I know that it went out on the prayer chain about Gracie Parks taking Tish Ball and Molly Maginnis to the emergency room this afternoon. I just want to reassure you that, although both were very sick when admitted, Molly was doing quite well when I left the hospital, just before coming here, and Tish, also, seems to be improving."

Gracie continued with her kitchen duties, sure that Rocky would be using all his reportorial skills trying to get answers to his many questions. But she was equally positive that

Herb was going to release only those facts he chose to.

She enjoyed the murmur of diners' conversations, the sudden bursts of laughter and the occasional louder voice of an individual entertaining his table with some story or teasing. These people knew one another well and took pleasure in being together, that she knew.

Thank You, Lord, that I've been able to stay here in Willow Bend during my entire married life — even after my beloved El's death. These are my people, and I love them.

As her helpers brought back the serving dishes for the final time, she began combining leftovers in their respective containers — stuffing, potatoes, ham, chicken, vegetables, salad — and asked Marge to make the announcement she would have given under normal circumstances.

She deliberately stood behind Eleanor and Marge, who were both taller, when Bud Smith, the high school principal and this year's Rotary president, got to his feet and called everyone from the kitchen for a special thank-you, to be conveyed by applause.

But he then went on to declare that Gracie Parks deserved special appreciation because, on only a couple days' notice, she'd managed to get this marvelous meal together for them after the originally scheduled caterers were called away due to a family emergency.

She could no longer avoid the attention of the room, but she tried to conceal her face by ducking her head slightly. Then she realized she had nothing whatsoever to be ashamed of, even if she looked her worst. With pride, she raised her head high and announced, "If any members are ill or were unable to come, or if you have a shut-in neighbor who might enjoy a meal like the one you ate this evening, please raise your hand if you'd be willing to deliver a free take-out meal for them. We will have those ready for pick-up on your way out, after the program."

She hurried back to the kitchen and set about placing the foods in divided-compartment plastic boxes with attached lids. Stacking these in the refrigerator, she then picked up a towel and started to dry the washed pots and pans, and put them away.

But as she and the others heard snatches of the program, it sounded so interesting that they went out to watch the last part of "A Walk Down Willow Bend's Main Street," spotlighting the town of a century ago. She knew the speaker, of course: his ancestors had preceded him as owners of Robertson's Pharmacy, and Charley was using many of his dad's and grandfather's and great-grandfather's old photographs of local landmarks and people.

There were a number of well-received interruptions as people shared memories of stopping at the pharmacy for penny candy on their way home from elementary school, and of watching the old schoolhouse being torn down and then replaced with the big yellow-brick Willow Bend Bank.

Gracie returned to the kitchen just before the lights came back on in the big room to greet the individuals who'd reserved meals and now wished to pick them up. Most took the opportunity to try asking questions as to what had taken place concerning Tish and Molly.

She answered as briefly as possible. She didn't wish to seem to be attempting to withhold information, but even surrounded by so many friends and old acquaintances who wished her well, Gracie knew she must reply with caution.

The task of keeping her own counsel was starting to wear on her — and she wondered if her annoyance was evident to Herb, who walked down the hallway and came up to her, cell phone in hand.

"Can I speak with you for a minute, Gracie?"

Rescue!

Chapter Ten

Sighing, she moved over to join him. "Thanks, Herb. I couldn't get rid of them."

He went straight to the point. "Tish's fingerprints are on the doorjamb and on the back of a chair."

"Ah-ha! And Molly's?"

"At first she refused to give permission for us to take hers for a match — till we convinced her we were about to go over her head to obtain authorization. It finally got through to her that it was better to cooperate."

"Does she have a lawyer?"

"We've suggested that she get one, but thus far she hasn't, at least as far as I know."

They walked back toward the kitchen, where they found Rocky and Ben, obviously waiting for them. "Look, Gracie," Rocky said, "I've talked with Herb, and have agreed to let this story lie for twenty-four hours — but I do have a favor to ask."

Her glance toward Herb showed his face to be noncommittal, so she turned back to

Rocky. "I guess that depends on the favor — and whether it's tied into the deal you made with him."

"Right." He took her hand and squeezed it. "What I'd like is for you to permit Ben to take a couple pictures of you right here in the kitchen. Please. We'll have it in the file — and it's an important angle."

"I'd rather not."

"The story will run, Gracie. It's local news, big news, and it will have to. It's conceivable that it may even end up tying in with a certain missing-person file."

Gracie wondered how Herb managed to remain so expressionless. "I'd like to fade into the background in that case, Rocky."

"Okay." Rocky nodded, perhaps biding his time. "I spent over an hour this afternoon going through our records concerning Frank's disappearance — and concerning Molly's thus-far fruitless efforts to get him declared legally dead.

"She's insisted the process should be speeded up, that she's experiencing financial and emotional difficulties. And, of course, neither insurance company has paid off — not the one he had an average-sized policy with for thirty-four years nor the one taken out just the year before he disappeared — a much *larger* one."

"I hadn't realized that."

"We learned of those attempts while making routine checks at the courthouse." Wrinkles formed across his forehead as his eyebrows lifted close to his unruly salt-and-pepper hair. "Perhaps wrongly — if today's suspicions prove accurate — I made the decision not to publish that."

There was silence for a few seconds before Gracie remarked, "That's a lot of wooded area out there to search through years later."

This time it was Herb who heaved a sigh. "It sure is!"

Uncle Miltie came to the kitchen as Gracie entered with the first load of leftovers. "It's a mighty good thing the electricity's back on!"

She could smile about it now. "Had it not been, these would have remained at the church."

She went back out, and he held the screen door open for her as she returned with her arms again full. "This is all of the perishables. The rest can stay in the car till morning."

"You can't expect all this to fit in your refrigerator!"

"Of course I do! In the morning I'll

package much of it for freezing, but for tonight these containers will fit once I put the stuffing and potatoes and salads in plastic bags so they'll fit on top of or squeezed between other items."

He stayed in the kitchen while she organized the storage, and he was furiously indignant at the physical threat his niece had been forced to endure. He was still angry when he returned to the other room to finish a mystery novel he'd started several days earlier.

Gracie found herself to be utterly exhausted, and it wasn't long before she wished him good night and got ready for bed. She glanced at the Sunday School materials on the stand, but decided she needed rest even more than preparation for her class.

Yet she had trouble dropping off. She told herself that must be because she usually went to sleep while lying on her right side, which she couldn't manage tonight, with her cheek hurting so much. It was much later when she admitted to herself that the problem might be due to all that adrenaline her body had been churning out throughout this day.

Morning came too soon. She started to

roll over again, but stopped in time. *It's hard to remember not to lie on my right side — and it's not fun having the left side of my face hurting even more than the right one — undoubtedly because Molly's right-handed.*

But I don't want to get up yet! I'm as tired now as when I went to bed — and was hoping for so much more sleep! That didn't seem likely, with her mind still as charged up as before. She couldn't help trying to determine which of her imagined scenarios concerning Molly might prove to be correct.

And it could be none of these. She and Frank did always seem to have totally different perspectives about things, but could she have been so hate-filled that she'd kill him?

Or so greedy?

She finally turned on her bed-light to begin reading Sunday's lesson. It was well-written and, under ordinary circumstances, would have held her interest. Then she tried reading the latest issue of *Guideposts*. But her thoughts were still spinning around. She finally gave up trying, however, and, this time more carefully, rolled onto her left side.

She was up and in the kitchen by six, preparing and marking two-portion packages. She often cooked extra-sized meals for her uncle and herself, so she'd have a second, or even a third meal all ready to thaw and reheat. What she was doing this morning was what she often did — make similar use of her catering leftovers.

Some things couldn't be frozen, so she filled several pint containers with coleslaw, and put into plastic bags what tossed salad she wouldn't be able to use up within the next day or two. Fortunately, her son Arlen loved her coleslaw and when he arrived on Saturday would make a serious dent in the leftovers. These and the extra homemade rolls were taken with her as she started off for a three-mile walk. She didn't stop to visit, but on her way did the rounds of some of Eternal Hope's more elderly members, asking their help in eating up these extras.

She disposed of everything within the first half-hour, completing the rest of her jaunt more briskly for being empty-handed. Uncle Miltie was waiting at the door when she got back, eager to report that she'd had a number of phone calls.

The one she chose to return first was Tish, still at the hospital. "Good morning. How are you today?" *And thank You, God,* she breathed.

"Much better than yesterday — though I don't remember much of that."

"What do you recall?"

"Before I get into that, there's something else I want to say. I understand that you saved my life, and I need to thank you, very much."

"You're more than welcome, dear. I'm so very, very grateful that I was able to get there in time!" Then, not wanting to be forced to recount her own role in any detail, she again asked, "What I need to learn is what you recall from yesterday."

"Well-l-l, I'm going to start back a little way. I'd been driving after dark the night Marge's hydrangeas were stolen, and as I turned the corner by your house my car lights showed Molly right there by those flowers. I had the impression, with my first glance, that she was cutting them, but then she — seemed to be trying to keep from being seen, or at least recognized, for she turned away.

"This seemed odd, but I told myself to forget it. And pretty much I did until the following morning, when I heard about Marge's flowers being stolen. I was almost positive that was what Molly had been up to, but I might not have done anything about it had I not then learned what happened with all those others from our church — and even from Eternal Hope itself!"

There was a little pause, but Gracie didn't

want to intrude if her friend was getting her thoughts and memories in order. Tish finally went on, "I figured I had to let her know I'd seen her — and that I expected her to make apologies to each of those people."

"So you went over to her house and . . . ?" Gracie left that open-ended.

"Yes. It was such a pretty day I decided to walk over. At first Molly pretended not to know what I was talking about. But when I told her the exact time I'd seen her and everything, she admitted I was correct. Only about Marge's, though.

"What especially bugged me was her sort of shrugging off any sense of guilt, not seeing any reason to apologize. But when she finally realized I wasn't about to drop the matter, she said she'd do as I requested — as I *demanded*.

"So then she seemed to feel fine about the situation. In fact, she insisted I stay for some freshly made iced tea and cookies."

"And you . . . did."

"Well, I didn't actually want to fake a friendship I no longer felt, but told myself that staying long enough for a glass of tea was the least I could do since she'd agreed to make that apology." Her voice seemed to fade out a bit, then get stronger, "I said I'd take a pass on the cookies, though.

"So she brought in a full glass of some kind of herbal tea. I wasn't sure. It was more than I wanted, but she kept saying to drink a little more. And I did."

"It — tasted all right?"

"It was sweeter than I make it, and it may have had a slightly different flavor — Herb kept asking about that, too. I told him that if it was different, it wasn't unpleasant. The thing is, many commercially prepared tea drinks now have slightly varying flavors, especially all the herbal ones."

Yes, that's true. "So — you emptied your glass?"

"Um-hm. And Molly took it right to the kitchen, and rinsed it out."

"She didn't — actually wash it, or put it in the dishwasher?" *Perhaps this can still be checked by the authorities.*

"I think she set it in the dish drainer, or maybe in the sink."

What else should I be asking? "I take it you were right there in the kitchen with her, since you remember seeing her rinse out the glass."

"Yeah — and that's when I saw those *hundreds* of hydrangeas out there in her sunroom!

"When I asked about them, she said she had contacts with other growers who were trying to develop new varieties. She even took me out there and told me the names of dozens of them, and pointed out the slight differences in color or size or number of blooms.

"I'll admit to being suspicious as to where some of those cut ones in the buckets and other large containers came from, but by then I just wanted to get away from there." She sighed. "Stan says that if I'd kept my mouth shut at that time, Molly might not have kidnapped me as she did."

"But — hadn't she already given you that drink? I'd be more apt to suspect her of deliberately keeping you there till that potion took effect."

"I think so, too — now," she agreed, "and so does Herb. I was getting drowsy and, looking back on it, I suspect my tripping over a bucket and sloshing water on one of her throw rugs was probably due to that!"

"Then what happened?" Gracie prodded, breaking Tish's lengthening pause.

"Things are sort of fuzzy from there on, but then I thought it was nice of Molly to say she had to run an errand anyway, so we'd just go out to the garage, so she could drive me home."

Gracie didn't nudge her this time; she could wait any amount of time for what was coming. "I just vaguely recall getting in her car — and her suggesting that I lie down on the backseat, which I did. And then she put some sort of a blanket over me. . . .

"But — I have no memory at all of arriving out at the cabin, even though Herb says I must have been able to stand and walk — probably with her help, though. And I don't remember your arriving or the drive back, or Les being there, or anything else until I woke up here." Tish gave a small gulp. "It's too weird."

Gracie swallowed hard. "Well, it was lucky we got you to the emergency room in time! But more than luck, I'm sure it was all the praying I did!"

"I've thanked God a good many times today, myself." But then she asked, "It didn't occur to me until after Herb left, but how did you know to check for me at *Molly's?* And to go out there to the cabin looking for me?"

Gracie briefly filled her in as to Uncle Miltie's seeing her — or Tyne — go into the Maginnis house that morning — and Tish's having written Molly's number on her phone pad.

After this, Gracie paused for a pick-me-up, treating herself to some fresh-squeezed orange juice before she began returning the other calls. Eventually she got around to phoning Carter, who made it clear that the Willow Bend crisis had claimed more of her thoughts since yesterday than she'd given to her own responsibilities in Chicago! "I just can't trust you to stay out of trouble there, Aunt Gracie," she chided affectionately.

Gracie sank down onto a kitchen chair and propped her feet on the one next to it. "It does seem that way, doesn't it? And here I am, trying my best to behave!"

"That'll be the day!" Her niece laughed. "When I called, it was to make sure you're okay — and that the patients are doing all right."

"Yes, and yes," she responded. "I talked with Tish a little while ago, and found that she may even be leaving the hospital this afternoon."

"Great! Anyone who doesn't consider that a miracle sure doesn't recognize one when she sees it!"

It was another few minutes before Carter asked, "Just for the record, is anyone any closer to knowing whether Frank Maginnis did just disappear?"

"I understand there are two or three teams out there in the woods today, guided by specially trained dogs."

To learn more, Gracie would have to

check with Herb Bower. She dialed the police station and was told he wasn't in but would be later.

The fact that she was unusually restless all day should have come as no surprise. Uncle Miltie, too, felt the strain and kept coming out to the kitchen while she was working there, then followed her to the side yard when she went to weed one of the flower beds.

"I wonder," he said, not looking at her as he snipped off another spent rose, "how the flower judging went at the fair this morning."

She kept on working. "Probably a lot of the same winners."

He moved his walker just a little closer. "In some of the categories, no doubt."

She didn't choose to mention hydrangeas either. "Would you like to ride over to the fairgrounds?"

He shook his head. "Not today. But how 'bout just walking around a few blocks — you know, getting the blood circulating?"

She almost mentioned that she'd already done that this morning, but remembered he had not. She wanted to finish making this bed weed-free, but knew she needed to reassure him with her company. "That sounds like a great idea."

"And I'll treat you to a milkshake or whatever if you're up to stopping at The Sweet Shoppe or Jamie's Dairy," he promised.

I know, you're thinking it could be good for me to get away from the house, perhaps talk face to face with other people. But I'll let you think I don't catch on to your way of trying to help. "I'd rather just do some walking, if that suits you."

He didn't look in her direction as he clipped off another flower. "Sure — as long as you're not staying away from folks because you're embarrassed about your appearance."

So that's what's bothering him! "If I were that easily upset, my dear uncle, I wouldn't have shown up last night for that dinner! And stood up then in front of everyone."

"Oh, yes, you would!" he corrected. "If there was ever someone with an overdeveloped sense of duty, it's you. Once you gave your word about catering that meal, there was no way you'd ever back out!"

"Well-l-l. . . ."

"I do love and respect you for being like that, Gracie." He reached to place his gnarled hand on her head as she knelt there by the flower bed. "But please, next time take better care of yourself. When I think

195

that I — that we might have lost you, it makes cold chills run up my spine."

She looked into his loving, eighty-year-old blue eyes and smiled through the mist that clouded her own. Getting to her feet, she gave him a quick hug and, determined to lighten the mood, said, "I'll be ready to leave for that chocolate-peanut-butter milkshake in about three minutes."

They started off as a twosome, but Gooseberry, who'd seemed asleep while lying under some phlox plants, got up, stretched and joined them. They took their time all along the way, stopping to admire several outstanding and favorite gardens and individual plants or groupings, as well as a few newly painted houses.

She got her special milkshake and sipped it slowly as they sat in the front booth of The Sweet Shoppe. When Uncle Miltie had finished his bowl of butter pecan ice cream with chocolate syrup dribbled over it, they started for home. She took her drink with her and had it almost finished when they got to the street just before Molly's.

Gooseberry, who had been just in front of them, paused just long enough to look in each direction before, tail and head high, walking on across.

Gracie called to him, but was ignored,

and Uncle Miltie asked her, "You know why he crossed the street, don't you?"

"No, I don't!" she retorted. "He. . . ."

Her uncle went on, "Because the chicken's on vacation."

She saw the twinkle in his eyes and laughed with him. "You got me on that, Uncle Miltie — one of the oldest jokes in the world!" But she appreciated his trying to lift her spirits.

They had followed Gooseberry and were now at the beginning of the stone wall fronting Molly's property.

She started to pass by, but it was the place her uncle usually stopped to rest on the way home, so she wasn't surprised when he sat down, saying, "I wonder whether, when building this, they expected it to be used as a resting-place. It couldn't be better."

Perched beside him, Gracie kept an eye on her cat, still meandering along. "Do you suppose Molly will get to come back here — to enjoy all of this?"

"Well, they did let her return for now on — what's it called? Released on her own recognizance! Actually, that's a better break than I think she deserves."

"There's a major difference legally between attempting a murder and accomplishing it. And I expect she will show up for that hearing — I can't imagine her forfeiting such a huge amount of money — which is what would happen if she doesn't!"

She looked around. "You know, I think Molly's looking out of her living room window. I'm almost sure I saw movement there."

He nodded and turned to wave in that direction before pulling his walker closer and pushing himself back up onto his feet. "I'm rested enough, anyway." They'd gone only as far as the walk leading to her front door before he glanced toward the house again. "This house has such nice clean lines — or did till Molly added that box of a garage!"

That comment doesn't surprise me. I often heard about all the excellent advice Miltie used to give to people who hired him thinking he was merely a contractor, then learned better. "She likes the convenience of the attached garage — but I agree, the house looked more beautiful, much classier before." *And that "convenience" was one thing that made it possible for her to spirit Tish away.*

But then she had another thought, which was so far-out she hesitated even to mention it. "Uncle Miltie . . . ?"

"What?"

"We were talking about this recently, but why do you suppose Molly leaves that shell of a garage there in her yard? She had the remains of the roof and doors and stuff hauled away but — well, I suppose it would have cost a lot more to have what's left of those walls taken down and the cement blocks removed."

"And the foundations dug up and hauled away. You wouldn't want to have to mow around them if the rest was gone."

"That's true." They walked on a little further. "Her garage floor wasn't cement like ours so, since the roof was gone, it was easy for her to plant those vines to climb the walls inside and out. And — it doesn't look too bad in the summertime, like this."

"But it sure doesn't add to the beauty or value of the property."

She stopped there in the middle of the sidewalk, unable to see Gooseberry. "You can go on if you'd like, but the third member of our family seems to be missing again."

He rolled his eyes. "And, of course, he's much too independent to come if you call him. Unless he suspects there might be food in the offing."

Gracie started back and, seeing the big orange cat inside what was left of that garage, crossed the grass to get him. *He's probably hunting something — maybe even saw it come in here.*

The front door opened and Molly stormed out. "You've got a lot of nerve, Grace Parks, trespassing here after all you've already done!"

Gracie forced herself to speak calmly. "I just came to collect my cat, Molly. He was walking with my uncle and me until he wandered off."

Molly planted herself at the front corner of her house, her fists on her hips and a scowl on her face, watching Gracie lift Gooseberry in her arms and walk back across the yard. Gracie put the squirming creature down and called out, "I hope the rest of your day is nice, Molly."

The woman, chin tilted upward, turned on her heel and marched back inside, slamming the door for emphasis.

Gracie didn't like her thoughts, but might have discussed them with her uncle if, just as she reached him, Tyne Anderson hadn't pulled over to the curb and hurried from the car. "I just have to thank you again, Gracie!" Her arms went around her friend, and hugged her tightly. Then she turned and scooted back to her car. "Bye!"

They called their good-byes back to her, and Uncle Miltie chuckled. "That's got to be the shortest conversation that woman has ever had."

And Gracie nodded.

"Perhaps she's on her way to the hospital to be with Tish, or maybe even to help John move her back home."

There was a message on the answering machine that Herb had called back and, since he needed to go out again, would be in touch later.

Above the phone was that beautifully embroidered, framed sampler Elmo's grandmother had made as a girl. Gracie knew by heart each of *The Parks Family's Five Rules to Live By*, but for the umpteenth time she read with pleasure, "God keeps life mysterious but that doesn't mean you should stop trying to figure it out."

That seemed funny when I first saw it, but I now recognize the truth in it. Sometimes we seem to have to do more "figuring" than others — like right now when I've got this persistent feeling, this strong sense of being on the edge of understanding, that with a little more thinking about it and a whole lot more prayer, this situation with Molly is going to make sense.

This reminded her of being at the mall and finding she'd left behind on the refrigerator the list of all those things she needed or wanted to take care of. There had to be important things she wasn't remembering, or else not seeing in the right relationship with one another.

In some corner of her mind had to be the hint she needed — that clue still beyond recognition. Often, when she was troubled like this, she'd make some complicated new recipe, or bake pies, or cookies — anything that kept her hands busy but somehow seemed to free up her mental processes.

But we still have one and a half pies — actually a variety of leftover pieces brought home in two pie pans — and, although I gave away most of the rolls, there are eight of them left. So there's no point in making more of anything along that line.

She went outside again — just in time for Gooseberry to proudly bring his latest trophy — a dead mole — and lay it at her feet. She dutifully leaned over and petted him, telling him what a great hunter he was and that she was glad this particular critter wasn't going to be eating her bulbs anymore.

"And another commendable thing, Gooseberry, is your not letting my taking you from hunting at Molly's discourage you. No, you just came home and did your thing here."

Perhaps I should be as single-minded as you.

And then, then it finally came to her, that conversation from the past that might very well contain the clue she had been seeking.

Chapter Eleven

She called the police station and learned that Herb had returned, however, he was on the phone. "Do you know if he's planning to leave again right away?"

"Not that I know of, Gracie — but that's a possibility with each incoming call." This was Gladys Newforth, the part-time clerk.

"Yes, of course."

"I do know he's planning to call you."

"If at all possible, keep him there for a bit — don't let him leave immediately, okay? I'm gonna drive over there right now."

Gladys laughed. "I'll do my best!"

Gracie shouted out to her uncle that she had an errand to run, but would be back shortly, then quickly left before he had a chance to ask questions. She pulled into the station's parking lot within a few minutes and entered the office. She didn't get to sit down in the waiting room, however, for she was waved back to the inner one.

Herb got to his feet to greet her with,

"Well, Gracie, we finally manage to get together on this busy day."

She nodded. "As Uncle Miltie would say, 'If ya keep tryin' long enough, you're sure to get something, even if it's just a callus.' "

He didn't try to hide the smile in his eyes. "I'm not sure I relish being thought of as thick-skinned."

She gave a quick grin in response, which was gone by the time she dropped into a chair. "Are the searchers still out there in the woods?"

"Um-hm. And thus far have found nothing."

"What did Molly do or say when she found that search had begun?"

"It didn't seem to upset her." He shrugged. "And perhaps she really doesn't care what we do there — in which case we're using a lot of manpower on an incorrect and worthless guess."

"It — might also be possible that the guess is right, but the location isn't."

"Quite possible!" He sat there, head slightly cocked. "So what does that intuition of yours have to suggest as a better site?"

"Well, you remember that Elmo and Frank were very good friends, liked many of the same things and helped one another in different ways?"

He nodded and she went on, "I liked Frank, too — for that matter, everyone in the choir did. He had a good baritone voice, but we especially missed his personality when he was gone — that and his sense of humor.

"But he allowed Elmo to see the other side of him, the hurting and unhappy side. He and Molly didn't always get along too well, apparently, and every little thing seemed to become a major problem. Like that garage, for example.

"When they bought the place, there was only a very small, one-car garage back on the alley — and that's all they had for years because Molly insisted on a garage attached to the house, and he wanted it some distance away.

"Frank knew someone whose garage had gone up in a blaze before the fire company could even get there. These folks' attached house caught on fire — and their baby died.

"So Frank told Elmo he'd never sleep through the night if his garage was fastened to the house, and one year when Molly was visiting relatives, he just went ahead and had that big, cement-block, double-door one built, and the old one torn down and removed.

"Which started a major war when she returned."

Herb was frowning. "But —"

"To the best of my knowledge, she refused to use it even once until after he was gone. She'd just park in the driveway, even when it meant de-icing or removing snow from her car all during the winter."

"Really?" His frown indicated he hadn't known this.

"Then, later, after he was — gone, she used that garage all the time. Until it burned, that is, and she had the new one built right where she'd always wanted it.

"And she planted vines along the old masonry walls, and started an old-fashioned flower garden within it."

He cleared his throat as he uncrossed his long legs and reversed their position. "Your point being?"

"Well, Gooseberry left Uncle Miltie and me today to go over and check out that building — what's left of it — and that reminded me of those many times when he used to go there and sniff around and scratch and dig."

"So — what you're recommending is that we bring in some of the dogs to check right here in town?"

"It's only a suggestion, Herb. I could be way off."

He tightened his lips, though his expres-

sion wasn't really severe. "If I hadn't bene-
fited from a number of your previous
suggestions, I'd be a lot more skeptical."

"The other thing that makes me wonder is
that Molly was furious because I was on her
lawn and at that concrete-block shell today,
where I went to bring Gooseberry back.
And, by the way, she seems to think that all
the trouble she's in right now is my fault, as
you said."

He leaned forward. "Tell me, does your
cat — does Gooseberry seem to favor one
particular part of that former garage?"

"Yes, he does. But until today I'd assumed that was probably where he killed an
occasional mouse or something — maybe a
whole nest of them. It's usually the side far-
thest from the house, between the two windows."

He drew in a deep breath and let it out
slowly as he picked up the phone. "Strange,
isn't it, Gracie? Most people hope they're
right when they make decisions. As for me,
this time I'm hoping we're wrong!"

"Yes," she agreed. "I hope that, too. I
don't want to find that she's capable of
murder — that she has succeeded in doing
it! But she tried it with Tish and me, so,"
she paused as her fingertips gently touched
her cheeks, "it does seem possible."

Gracie listened as the arrangements were made, a little surprised at what was involved. She considered asking if she could tag along, but knew it was not her business — and that Molly would never, ever forgive her if she discovered Gracie had suggested that the police search her town property.

Nearing home, Gracie turned off to stop at the convenience store to pick up milk. She didn't need it right now, but she'd have to have some excuse to account for her absence. While there, she also got pretzels and a half-gallon carton of strawberry frozen yogurt, which might help keep her uncle from asking too many questions.

Barb Jennings was going through the check-out just in front of Gracie. She wanted to know, of course, about Gracie's scars. "They're nothing serious, and are already starting to heal," Gracie told her. "It was every bit as awful as I'm sure you've heard — but now I'm taking a break from thinking about it."

Barb, usually more intractable, immediately changed gears, saying she'd understood that Tish and Molly were doing so well that both were home now.

Gracie didn't mention to her uncle about going to the station, just said how busy the grocery store was — and he seemed satis-

fied. He proceeded to open the bag of pretzels and happily clomp off with a few of these looped around his fingers.

Several calls came during the evening, but none offered the information Gracie was waiting more and more impatiently to hear. It was not until the early morning newscast that she learned that the body of Frank Maginnis had been found, wrapped in plastic and buried in his own garage!

His wife — his widow, rather — had been taken into custody on suspicion of murder.

Uncle Miltie entered the kitchen, only to become upset at the sight of his niece sitting there at the kitchen table with tears running down her cheeks and an untasted cup of almost-cold tea on the table before her.

"What is it, Gracie?" He came to her as fast as he could move his walker. "What happened?"

She buried her face against his shirt and wrapped her arms around him. "It's Molly. She did kill him."

"She . . ." he had to clear his throat before going on, "whom did she kill?"

"Frank! She killed that wonderful man who was her husband," and she cried even harder. She'd considered the possibility and encouraged the authorities to do so. At the same time she hadn't wanted it to be true.

She'd gone out on a limb for Tish, and almost been killed by Molly but still hadn't wanted to believe the latter capable of the cold-blooded murder of her husband.

"So — he didn't just walk away."

"It never made sense that he had," she told him. "But her story seemed to be at least plausible, except to a few of us — and we didn't know what to do about it."

The phone rang, and Gracie just sat there, making no move to answer it. Uncle Miltie looked from her to it and back again, then took the few steps necessary to pick it up. "Hello?"

"It's Rocky. May I speak with Gracie?"

"I'll ask her. She just heard the news on the radio, and I'm not sure she'll want to talk even with you right now."

"In that case, I must talk to her. Please give her the phone — even if she says she doesn't want to talk to anyone."

He carried the cordless phone to the table. "It's for you, Gracie." She just shook her head, and he urged, "It's Rocky, and he says he has to talk with you."

"I can't — not now. . . ."

But he thrust the mouthpiece up close to her, so Rocky must have heard, since he was now speaking more loudly, "You were right, Gracie, right on the button!"

"I didn't want to be right!" It was almost a wail. "I — somehow feel responsible. . . ."

"You *were* responsible, that's the whole point!" His voice showed something she didn't quite recognize, not in this context. It sounded something like commendation, and he was saying, "You did what had to be done, Gracie, no matter how painful that was — and your poor face is proof of that!

"You're the one responsible citizen who has made it possible for her to get stopped before anyone else was killed."

She'd never been a person who coveted praise, but it helped that this man she liked and respected so much thought she'd done the right thing. "Do they think there could be — others?"

She hadn't been able to fit words together to be more specific than that, but those were apparently enough. "We have no way of knowing right now, Gracie. Both Herb's sources and mine are checking to see if there are other mysterious disappearances that might conceivably be connected with her, not only here but throughout the state — or elsewhere."

"Has she admitted to killing Frank?"

"No, and probably won't — not now, anyway. She doesn't yet have her own defense lawyer, and the state-appointed one will almost surely advise against her admitting to anything at this stage."

They talked a little more before he asked, "How about my picking you up in fifteen or twenty minutes and taking you out for breakfast?"

"I — don't think I could eat enough to make it worthwhile, Rocky, but thanks. I'm not hungry."

"Me neither — for food. But it seemed a good excuse to sit face to face and just be two old friends taking time to be together."

"I don't feel up to seeing anyone, even you."

She expected that to take care of the matter, but it didn't. Rocky pulled up at the house shortly after that — inviting himself to have coffee with Uncle Miltie. They also finished the last three pieces of cherry pie before he left for the *Gazette* office.

They talked no more about Molly, and Gracie told him quite truthfully as he left that he was very good medicine. Overhearing that, Uncle Miltie informed him in a loud aside that she hadn't mentioned what kind or *flavor* of medicine she was referring to. "Some are purely horrible, even if they're good for you, so don't get too swell-headed."

Rocky was smiling as he went out the door, probably appreciating the fact that

Gracie had stepped outside to wave at him as he left. He would have grinned even more broadly had he known what she was thinking. *What a fine man he is! Even with all he has to do, he took time to come over to give me the help he thought I needed!*

You know, Gracie, if you are ever to fall in love again, I hope it will be with someone like him.

She'd never had that thought in her mind before, not consciously, anyway. *And you're not looking for love, that kind of love. After Elmo, anyone else would be a disappointment.*

But was that true?

She didn't know whether Rick Harding had planned to stop, but he pulled over to the curb when he saw her working outside. "Did you see the listings in today's paper of the County Fair's prizewinners?"

She shook her head. "Miltie brought it in, but I haven't looked at it yet. And I presume you're thinking of hydrangeas?"

"I sure am! They were the only category I had time to check."

"And . . . ?"

"Every single one of those winners is from out of town this year!"

"Did even one of us from town enter? I didn't — did you?"

He shook his head. "All of mine that might have had a chance of winning, those mini-ones, were removed — as was the case with yours and those at the church and Barb's —"

"Hey, you two!" Uncle Miltie had come to the screen door. "You may not have won any prizes this year, but you sure as shootin' didn't lose, either!"

"That's true, Uncle Miltie, my dear, very true," she agreed. "And so, uncowed and unbeaten, we will continue to work on our hydrangeas, propagating those posies and wowing those judges next year!"

Gracie had raised her right fist in the time-honored gesture of the challenger. "Watch for us next year, Willow Bend, you're going to see some winners!"

None of the three had any doubts about that.

Recipe

Gracie's Cheese Casserole (with macaroni)
(Quick but delicious)

1/2 cup margarine
1 pound uncooked macaroni
4 cups grated cheese (Cheddar,
    Parmesan, Swiss or other)
6 to 7 cups milk

Melt margarine in bottom of 9 x 13-inch pan. Add uncooked macaroni and stir until coated. Sprinkle grated cheese over surface. Pour in milk. Bake at 350 degrees for approximately 1 hour. Let sit for 10 to 15 minutes to become firmer.

Please note: I sometimes brown a pound of hamburger, then drain and add it to the mixture before baking. Delicious! You can also add onions and/or peppers — but Uncle Miltie prefers it plain.

About the Author

Words have always been a joy to EILEEN M. BERGER, who learned to read at an early age and could lose herself in books and magazines, particularly fiction. Raised on a poultry farm, she spent many hours alone, feeding and watering chickens and gathering eggs, and during those hours she often reimagined the plots of existing novels she had read and played with what-ifs.

"What if the author had done such-and-such in that third chapter, *then* what would have happened?" she'd ask herself. Or, "Suppose the author's lead male had a different personality or background, *then* how would the young woman react if he did the same — or other things?" From there it was a natural step to telling herself her own stories, or to promising herself to be an author someday.

But she lived for many years and through many experiences before disciplining herself to write down her thoughts, and in the meantime earned degrees from Bucknell and Temple universities — in biology, chemistry and medical technology. She became head of a pathology laboratory in a large Midwestern city before returning to Philadelphia to work toward an advanced degree — but then she fell in love with a young Baptist minister, got married and went to live in a tiny parsonage in a small north-central Pennsylvania town.

It was there, as a preacher's wife and mother, reading and telling hundreds of stories to the three little ones who soon came along, that she began writing and selling stories, poems and articles for children and adults. The books came later.

Eileen and Bob still live just outside of that same community, which they love. In addition to their church and community involvements, Eileen is active in various writers' organizations, especially the West Branch Christian Writers, the critique-support group she helped found twenty-some years ago, and St. Davids Christian Writers Association, which holds the second oldest annual conference for Christian writers in America.

The employees of Thorndike Press hope you have enjoyed this Large Print book. All our Thorndike and Wheeler Large Print titles are designed for easy reading, and all our books are made to last. Other Thorndike Press Large Print books are available at your library, through selected bookstores, or directly from us.

For information about titles, please call:
(800) 223-1244
or visit our Web site at:
www.gale.com/thorndike
www.gale.com/wheeler

To share your comments, please write:

Publisher
Thorndike Press
295 Kennedy Memorial Drive
Waterville, ME   04901

Guideposts magazine and the Daily Guide-posts annual devotion book are available in large-print format by contacting:
Guideposts Customer Service
39 Seminary Hill Road
Carmel, NY 10512
or
www. guideposts.com